FROELICH'S
LADDER

ADVANCE PRAISE

"*Froelich's Ladder* is a tall tale/fable/*kindermärchen* set in the Oregon Territory and featuring a large cast of eccentric characters. It's reminiscent of the works of Patrick deWitt, though entirely its own thing. I loved the magic and the tall tale-ness and the characters and I wish there were more books in the world that were creating new folklores and fairy tales. Sometimes we grown-ups need to be reminded of why we started loving stories in the first place, and *Froelich's Ladder* is a book that can do that."

    – Billie Bloebaum, bookseller, Third Street Books

"In *Froelich's Ladder*, Jamie Duclos-Yourdon debuts an impeccably crafted adventure in the best tall tale tradition. The men and women of his frontier Oregon are keenly drawn and brilliantly, painfully human, as is the book itself, touched with wit and whimsy and saturated with longing. Duclos-Yourdon's deft, lyrical prose gives the novel an impressive, addictive fairy-tale sensibility, and marks it as one of those rare reads that simultaneously evokes and transcends its wholly original time and place."

    – Tracy Manaster, author of *You Could Be Home by Now*

"*Froelich's Ladder* by Jamie Duclos-Yourdon is a modern fairy tale set during the pioneering days of Oregon. Modern and pioneering? Yes, just go with it; you won't be disappointed. Brothers Froelich and Harald have a fight that lasts decades and sends Froelich up the fourth-tallest ladder in the history of the world. There he stays and stays, until one day he is missing. An unbelievably charming story with the quirkiest of characters, *Froelich's Ladder* is required reading for Pacific Northwest lovers. Duclos-Yourdon clearly has a long career ahead of him."

    – Dianah Hughley, bookseller, Powell's Books

"Jamie Duclos-Yourdon's new novel, *Froelich's Ladder*, is the perfect tall tale for our time. Funny and smart, Duclos-Yourdon takes us back to just-settled Oregon. With logging camps, confederate spies, and industrious builders, this book is at once a lesson in Oregon history and a lesson in the unexpected. Overall, it's a joy to read; it's evocative of a different time, and a tale that's taller than the ladder Froelich builds."

– Kate Ristau, author of *Shadowgirl*

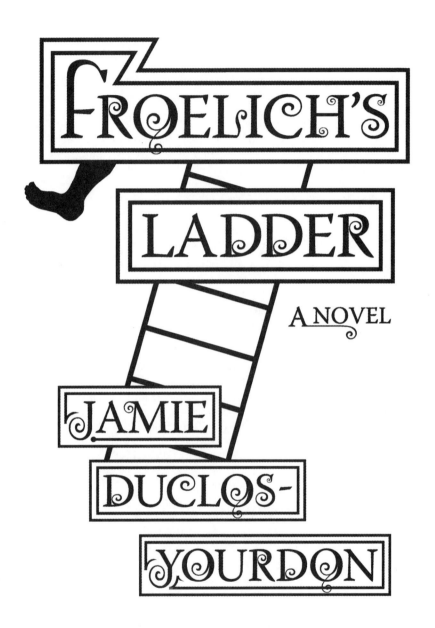

FROELICH'S LADDER

A NOVEL

JAMIE DUCLOS-YOURDON

FOREST
AVENUE
PRESS

Portland,
Oregon

An excerpt from *Froelich's Ladder* appeared in *Chicago Literati* in December 2014.

ISBN: 978-1-942436-19-5

Library of Congress Cataloging-in-Publication Data

Names: Duclos-Yourdon, Jamie, 1977- author.
Title: Froelich's ladder / Jamie Duclos-Yourdon.
Description: Portland, OR : Forest Avenue Press, 2016.
Identifiers: LCCN 2016010509 (print) | LCCN 2016021056 (ebook)
  | ISBN 9781942436195 (paperback) | ISBN 9781942436201 (ePub)
  | ISBN 9781942436218 (Kindle) | ISBN 9781942436225 (pdf)
Subjects: | BISAC: FICTION / Fairy Tales, Folk Tales, Legends
  & Mythology. | FICTION / Fantasy / Historical. | FICTION /
  Coming of Age. | FICTION / Literary.
Classification: LCC PS3604.U354 F76 2016 (print) | LCC PS3604.
  U354 (ebook) | DDC 813/.6--dc23
LC record available at https://lccn.loc.gov/2016010509

1 2 3 4 5 6 7 8 9

Distributed by Legato Publishers Group

Printed in the United States of America

Cover design: Gigi Little
Interior design: Laura Stanfill

Forest Avenue Press LLC
6327 SW Capitol Highway, Suite C
PMB 218
Portland, OR 97239
forestavenuepress.com

For Melissa:
every word

Now that my ladder's gone,
I must lie down where all the ladders start,
In the foul rag-and-bone shop of the heart.

– W. B. Yeats

CHAPTER 1

It was November 1851 when Harald and Froelich arrived in Oregon Country. Disembarking at Fort Astoria, they journeyed inland by foot, hiking over the Cascades in a gale that swept off the ocean like an enormous push broom. Above the eastern timberline, precipitation turned to hail—even masquerading as snow for one eerie afternoon, with flakes the size of dinner plates. When they finally descended and the land had leveled off, the air was buoyed by a gentle mist. Here, the hemlock trees were wrapped in wintergreen moss, unlike the whitebark pine they'd passed at higher altitudes, stooped over and rough to the touch.

Statuesque Harald was the picture of contentment, his eyes shut and his nostrils flared; unfortunately, his brother felt less rhapsodic. The third of four sons and heir to none of his family's fortune (which was comprised of a hog farm in Germany), Froelich had been born with outsized ambitions. He'd set his sights on America—convincing Harald, fourteen months his senior, to join him. But now the soles of Froelich's feet were soft and wrinkly from threadbare socks in sodden shoes. Loudly he complained, "I feel like an otter. Never in my life have I been so wet."

The brothers' land (two plots arranged end-to-end) was adjacent to Boxboro—less of a town at the time than the notion of a town. The previous year, the United States Congress had passed the Donation Land Act. Harald and Froelich, being of voting age and white (by accident of birth, and without conscious design), were entitled to three hundred twenty acres in Oregon Country, provided they make improvements to the land and remain for four years. At nineteen and eighteen years old, respectively, they received no greeting when they arrived, nor did anything but a handwritten mile marker signify their property.

"A bog," Froelich noisily observed. "It reminds me of a bog, Harald, only without the charm. In California, at least it's sunny. At least the people were civilized! Did you see that coot at the general store? His mouth looked like the back of your knee! Is it any wonder they're giving away land? If a person were to come up to you and say, 'Here, take my daughter—my pride and joy, a vision to see,' would you think to yourself, 'Oh lucky day!' Or would you think, 'Let me see this daughter of yours.' Maybe it's not even his daughter, Harald, but a man dressed as a woman, lying in wait! And when I pay her a visit, with my chin shaved and my hair nicely parted, he jumps out from behind the wardrobe, strikes me over the head, and—"

"Enough, Froelich!" Harald shouted, finally compelled to open his eyes. Staring down at his brother, he asked, "What are you trying to say?"

"What am I trying to say?" The volume of Froelich's voice was enough to startle the birds. "I'm saying it's abysmal here! I'm saying this has been a terrible mistake! No one should suffer such indignity, unless they're being punished for a grave sin—which, to my knowledge, I am not."

"But I *like* it here," Harald said. "I *enjoy* this weather."

"Don't be ridiculous," Froelich snapped. "Go live at the bottom of a well, if that's your preference. I say California was superior in every way. Or New Orleans—I rather liked the Port of New Orleans. Let's go back."

This statement caused Harald's jaw to swing open, as if on a great hinge. For a moment he was rendered speechless, his face all but frozen, except for a distressed vein that pulsed in his temple. Finally, when it appeared he might've been struck dumb, he offered a smile.

"Go back?" He chuckled.

"Yes—go back. What's so amusing?"

"Walk all the way to the Fort Astoria? And how will you, with your feet in that condition?"

Froelich folded his arms and scowled. He'd thought his limp was less noticeable, even as it had grown more and more pronounced. He felt it was cruel for Harald to make light of his affliction. After all, his brother stood head and shoulders above normal men and was strong as a locomotive.

"You'll have to carry me, of course," Froelich said.

Harald threw his head back as his laughter turned to howls. The rain dappled his forehead and ran in rivulets down his cheeks.

"Carry you?" he gasped, when he was finally able to speak.

Froelich, who was beginning to lose his patience, confirmed, "Yes—carry me. Don't pretend for a second that I'm too heavy."

"Of course you're not too heavy—I could put a wagon on my back. But why carry you? Why should I leave? This is my home now, Froelich. The contract requires that we stay for four years."

Now it was Froelich's turn to gape. The betrayal he felt stemmed less from what Harald wanted, and more from what he *didn't* want. Harald, with his unique physical gifts, could've made a name for himself in Deutschland, when no such option had been available to Froelich. *His* only chance at upward mobility had been to pursue his fortune, and that pursuit had led him to this wilderness.

"Come with me," Froelich said. "I want to show you something."

Technically, they were standing on Froelich's land. Slogging to the middle of an empty pasture, where the drizzle had turned the ground to slurry, he spun around to face his brother.

"There," Froelich said, pointing at his feet. Rain was dripping down his brow and under his collar, not that he noticed anymore. "Look right there, and tell me what you see."

"There?" Harald frowned. "All I see is mud."

"It's your grave," Froelich sneered. "Yours and mine, both—but you first, if rank stupidity has anything to do with it. We've traveled tens of thousands miles, Harald, and for what? The privilege of drowning while standing up? If that's the case, I'd rather spend what time remains alone. Oregon Country is big enough that I don't have to see your idiot face."

Hobbling toward the wall of the trees, he paused to correct himself. "*My* home," he said. "My land. You go live someplace else."

CHAPTER 2

Harald passed a peaceful fortnight, during which time he constructed a series of shelters, each one an improvement upon the last. He never left the pasture, as Froelich had instructed him—assuming, correctly, that his brother would return, and that they'd be forced to share accommodations. When Froelich did storm back, it seemed that little time had passed for all the respite he'd afforded.

Froelich had made two important discoveries on his own. First, he had discovered the Very Big Tree. After their dispute in the meadow, he'd spent three days limping through the woods, making his displeasure known to every living thing. When he'd encountered the tree, it had been so massive that he'd mistaken it for a rampart. Its trunk, felled by some catastrophe, was thrice as wide as he was tall. Froelich had spent a full morning walking along its length, from top (where birds continued to occupy their nests) to bottom (where the roots continued to grow). As best he could tell, it extended for a full kilometer.

To Harald's mind, the timber represented a commercial opportunity, but Froelich's second discovery, made shortly after the first, would supersede any material gain. In fact, it was this second discovery that had compelled him to seek his brother's help. Casting aside their differences, he hurried back to the pasture, where Harald was erecting yet another shelter.

"Love, Harald!" gushed Froelich, cheeks flushed and slightly out of breath. Harald saw that his limp had improved, perhaps due to a new pair of socks, expertly knit and dry as tinder.

"I'm in love!" he continued. "Here, at the bottom of the well, I've actually found it! What are the odds? Who would've thunk? Of course, you can't know how it feels until you've felt it for yourself. But simply to behold her, you might get the gist. She's the most beautiful girl I've ever seen, with hair as dark as night and eyes that smolder."

Harald wiped the sweat from his brow and put down his ax. In the time that his brother had been missing, Harald's frustration had subsided. Now, subject to Froelich's enthusiasm, he felt weary all over again.

"Did she give you those socks?"

"What?" Froelich said, frowning. "No, I got these in town. What are you talking about, socks? Haven't you heard a word I'm saying?"

"I'm sorry." Harald sighed, trying to muster some hint of enthusiasm. "What's her name?"

Her name was Lotsee, and she was an outcast from the Siletz tribe. At nineteen, she had entertained a premonition about her people: misery and death awaited them, to be nurtured in the too-small confines of the Coast Reservation (which would only be sanctioned four years later). Disinclined to share their fate, she'd swallowed her words of warning, chewing them up like tidy morsels. She'd left the Siletz and relocated to the outskirts of Boxboro.

Once she was on her own, Lotsee's visions hadn't ceased. Soon, she'd been forced to accept that Death would claim her, too, with or without her people. Her only hope, she'd believed, was to seduce him. To her mind, Death would resemble a white man, pale and hulking. If he were ruled by his baser instincts, surely he'd be in thrall to her charms.

All of this, related by the proprietor of the general store, Froelich now related to Harald. He felt confident he could win Lotsee's heart, but was embarrassed to approach her empty-handed. That, he explained, was where the Very Big Tree came in.

"Just look at this monster!" Froelich exclaimed, having convinced his brother to visit the enormous timber. "It must be a sign!"

"A sign of what?"

"Don't you see, Harald? It'll make the perfect engagement gift!"

"Engagement gift? All I see is an impediment."

"That's because you lack imagination."

"You want to chop it up for firewood?"

Froelich shook his head. "Yes, Harald—I want to give firewood to my bride-to-be. Before, when I said that you lacked imagination, I was mistaken."

"What, then?"

"A seafaring canoe—one big enough for twenty men!"

"No more boats," Harald groaned. "Anyway, what do you know about carving a canoe? Most likely it'll sink, and everyone on board it will drown."

"Then . . ." Standing back to better appraise the Very Big Tree, Froelich tapped a finger against the bridge of his nose. "I see . . . a ladder."

"A ladder?"

"Yes, a ladder! It'll be amazing, Harald, the tallest ladder you've ever seen! Not just the tallest in Oregon Country—possibly the tallest ladder in the entire world! A monument to human achievement! Can't you picture it?"

"What I can picture," Harald said, "is finishing our shelter, so we can spend the night in dry bedclothes. I can picture clearing the land and trading my services for a rooster and some hens. Would you like me to go on?"

"But, Harald, we must!"

"No, Froelich," Harald sighed, "we mustn't. I'm sure she's very pretty, and I can appreciate your desire to talk to her. But why not do that? Why not *talk* to her, instead?"

With a noticeable sag to his shoulders, Froelich

answered him. "Because anyone can talk to her. I must woo her."

"Woo, talk—what's the difference? All you do is introduce yourself."

"That's easy for you to say. Please, Harald. Help me do this, and I promise to leave you alone. No more favors. No more adventures."

And so Harald was duly persuaded. After all, how could he deny his brother, who was in thrall to the noblest of all emotions? Starting from the same place on the Very Big Tree and each working in opposite directions, they marked the first rung as the "middle" of the ladder—though whether their efforts would ultimately be equal, who could say? Each rung was three decimeters from the next, to be measured by the length of Froelich's forearm (Harald's arms being too burly for comparison), and slightly longer from stile to stile.

Early on, it was easy to exchange verses of song, or to speak. But as the days turned into weeks, and the brothers couldn't see or hear each other, the forest grew up between them. While they maintained separate campsites, they also developed a vocabulary called TAP. The language borrowed from Morse code, to which they'd been exposed on their transatlantic voyage, and used thumps and vibrations to form combinations of words. The time that elapsed between knocks determined the meaning of the word, or words, to be conveyed. For instance, one knock immediately followed by a second knock meant *Yes*. One knock gradually followed by a second knock meant *No*. Two knocks in a row meant *Good afternoon*.

Three knocks in a row meant *Rain.* Two knocks followed by a pause followed by a single knock meant *Perhaps, but it depends on the weather.* Three knocks, followed by a pause, followed by six knocks, followed by a pause, followed by four knocks meant, *Just because it rained to-day doesn't mean it will rain tomorrow—and should it rain tomorrow, you can't claim to have predicted it, simply on the basis of having said, "It feels like rain tomorrow."* And so on, and so forth. Even while they were apart, they were never truly alone.

For Froelich, progress guided him in the direction of Boxboro, which, at the time, consisted of a gristmill and a general store. At first, he only visited to acquire supplies, but soon he was inventing reasons to stay. On a humid night, he might linger by the general store and drink from the proprietor's flask. When homesteaders passed through, he'd portray himself as the mayor and stand upon whatever stump was tallest. Or if a different mood possessed him, he'd scale the nearest tree, brandish his hairless a—, and moan like a woebegone ghost.

At the same time, Harald was striving the opposite direction, driving himself deeper and deeper into the woods. The Very Big Tree hewed a path to Lotsee's meadow, wherein one day she was hanging her laundry out to dry. When he stumbled through a clutch of boysenberries she spun around, startled by the sound of his glottal invective.

Harald had yet to see Lotsee for himself, having relied on Froelich's description. At first glance, she was lovely. More than lovely—Lotsee was stunning. Harald was old enough to have known the caress of a woman; indeed, had he remained in Germany, he might've taken a wife already. But despite his impressive stature and his experience with the fairer sex, Harald was a shy individual at heart.

Cowed by Lotsee's beauty and mindful of his brother's claim, he took a good, long look then retreated to the woods. Soon thereafter, he regretted his decision to flee. He couldn't casually return to the meadow, which meant he'd lost a day's work. Worse yet, he'd failed to introduce himself! He hadn't even said hello! Instead, he'd hollered obscenities. Of course, Lotsee didn't know he was Froelich's brother; Froelich hadn't introduced himself yet. But whenever they *did* meet, she'd assume that Harald was crude and uncouth, if not a little touched in the head—a first impression that galled him to the bone.

Out of embarrassment, he neglected to tell Froelich. Some days had passed since their last correspondence via TAP; what Froelich didn't know, Harald decided, wouldn't hurt him. Additionally, he resolved never to utter another word to Lotsee—not the next time he saw her, nor ever. With any luck, she'd mistake him for a deaf mute.

The next day, when he returned to the meadow, the Very Big Tree was awaiting him . . . and so was Lotsee. She'd been attired in sensible clothing the day before, while conducting her chores, but now she wore a skirt and a blouse, and her hair (modestly threaded with silver) was arranged in a fastidious plait. Harald studiously avoided eye contact, busying himself with the rung at hand.

"Do not pretend you cannot see me, when you are standing in my shadow."

Harald froze, his shoulders tensed.

"Fine, then." She shrugged. "Pretend."

Lotsee crossed the short distance that separated them. When she sashayed her hips, the motion was like wading into deep waters.

"I know who you are," Lotsee said. "You are Death. You look as I expected, but it didn't stop me from being afraid. Had you beckoned to me yesterday, I would have gone with you willingly. I would have greeted my ancestors in the afterlife and endured their chiding. 'What, child,' I can hear them saying, 'did you really expect him to take a bride? When the sun shines down from the sky, is that for you, too?'"

Glancing at her sideways, Harald made no indication that he was able to understand her, nor that he'd even heard her. When she drifted closer, he could smell the lilac water on her skin. He was terrified he'd miss the chisel with his hammer and smash one of his fingers.

"When you left," Lotsee continued, "I was relieved. I was so happy to be alive! But soon I became irritated. *Why* did you not beckon to me? Was I not good enough for you? Then I looked down at my clothes—pants, like a man. My face, hands, and feet covered in dirt. That night, I talked to my ancestors again. I told them, 'Death thinks he can ignore me, just because he walks between the raindrops? You tell Death I would rather kiss a toad!' And here you are. So I ask you, Death—do I look better?"

Rather than acknowledge her, Harald coaxed a shape from the wood, a mound of sawdust growing at his feet. But Lotsee would not be ignored. Leaning forward and cupping his chin with her palm, she turned his face to her own. Thus compelled, he looked at her—truly looked at her. Immediately, his mouth filled with praise, everything from German poetry to American slang. He could imagine sharing a future together, one that didn't include Froelich: native daughters with matching plaits, and a raised ceiling for Lotsee's lean-to. Determined that he not voice these ideas, Harald pressed his lips together and shut his eyes.

Grunting at his intransigence, Lotsee walked behind his back and addressed his profile, the long expanse of the Very Big Tree laid out before them. "You are making a ladder?" she said. "Where will you take it, when you are finished?"

Her questions (and his inability to answer them) made him feel stupid. Opening one eye and then the other, he continued to work, chiseling twice as hard and twice as fast. Shavings floated on the breeze, coating his chest and shoulders. Though he was facing straight ahead, all he could see were Lotsee's eyes—not brown, as he might've expected, but gray like goosedown.

"It's a wedding present," he abruptly informed her. He didn't mean to ruin Froelich's surprise, but there it was.

Lotsee's response was curious. At first she stiffened,

but then she made a resigned sound, as if this were something she had already expected. Lightly, she placed her hands over his. Harald didn't know how to receive her touch. He looked everywhere but directly at her. Sawdust clung where it had alighted on his beard, making his neck itch. When she urged him to his feet and pulled him, step by step, in the direction of her lean-to, he was unable to resist. She was radiant and indefatigable. She was intended for his brother, but she had chosen him.

After their tryst had begun, Harald made a modest effort to contact Froelich. Over the next few days, he sent polite inquiries via TAP and even walked a short distance along the Very Big Tree, but he never pursued his brother as far as Boxboro, unwilling to stray from Lotsee's company. She and Harald spent nearly all their time together, caressing each other's bodies when they were within reach and gazing at each other when they were not.

Finally, once Harald had resigned himself to the inevitable consequences, he freed the finished portion of the ladder from the Very Big Tree. He left a considerable portion of the timber unmolested—nearly four hundred meters, by his estimate. If Froelich had intended the ladder as an engagement gift, Harald's thinking went, he might abandon his proposal upon discovering it missing; then the lovers could reveal themselves in the fullness of time. Employing a system of ropes and pulleys, Harald dragged it to the edge of the clearing, whereupon he'd constructed an enormous fulcrum—also carved from the Very Big Tree, and nearly his own height. To

Harald, it looked like a giant doorstop. Using this device as a wedge, he was able to erect the ladder, such that it could stand against the fulcrum without any assistance. At Harald's best estimate the stiles were seventy meters tall, gently wobbling like a newborn fawn.

It was breathtaking to behold—but that's not what Froelich saw when he emerged from the woods. What he saw was Harald and Lotsee, standing together in the shadow of the latticework. It was a scene of perfect contentment: Lotsee resting her head against Harald's chest, his arms wrapped around her, the two of them entwined like a solitary figure. It was enough to make Froelich retch, and so he did.

Before Harald could speak, Froelich had fled back to the woods—all the way to Boxboro, where he got terrifically drunk. Harald knew better than to pursue him. Froelich would return when he was good and ready. Whether he'd provoke a confrontation, or laugh about the affair, Harald couldn't say.

The next morning, when Harald quit Lotsec's bed, he went to inspect the fulcrum. He'd dreamed of stags during the night and planned to emboss the unfinished wood. But when he touched the stiles, he felt a curious vibration, like a TAP conversation already underway:

—*my own brother, as if it weren't bad enough. But for that swine to betray me, that duplicitous, bovine Judas—*

Froelich? Harald said, rapping his knuckles against the ladder. *Are you up there?*

—*me, who saved him from a life of boredom and hog s—t! Who loved him first among all men, even myself!*

Looking up, Harald could see nothing. Froelich had climbed so high that even the soles of his feet were no longer visible. Circling to the other side of the fulcrum, Harald grasped a rung in either hand, briefly considering his own ascent. But he was concerned that two men (one significantly larger than the other) might be too much weight for the ladder to bear. So instead he said, *Froelich, come down.*

No—I'd rather stay up here. Go enjoy your freedom, why don't you? Go and pick some berries to shove in your stupid mouth.

I will not, Harald replied. And because they were communicating in outsized gestures, he rashly contributed one of his own. Positioning himself opposite the fulcrum, with knees bent and shoulders hunched, he pulled the rungs toward him, straining with all his might, until the full heft of the ladder was leaning against his back.

What was that? Did you move the fulcrum?

Indeed I did. Now you can punish me for as long as you like, Harald vowed, his arms trembling from the effort. *I will not move until you come down.*

Then you'll have to wait a very long time, Froelich retorted. Which was true: Harald would wait there all day long, while Lotsee marveled at his stubbornness. Could Death himself be as obstinate as a Deutschman? The summer months waned, passing into autumn, and gradually a full year elapsed. In time, thanks to Lotsee's persistence and ingenuity, Harald's sons were born— also spaced fourteen months apart, the second of whom would leave him a widower. For the next seventeen years he would patiently wait, until a chance accident would take his life—and even then Froelich would stay up the rungs.

But now Harald muttered to himself, "A very long time is no time at all." Realizing he'd spoken aloud, he repeated the sentiment via TAP, flexing his knees and patiently waiting for Froelich's reply.

CHAPTER 3

It was a June morning in 1871 when Froelich disappeared. Dawn had erased the stars from the sky, and a rosy shoal of clouds was swimming toward the coast. Not until he woke did Binx, the younger of Harald's two sons, first notice a difference.

The ladder was light against his back. Yawning, Binx examined this sensation. Even without ballast, the ladder continued to move, its stiles tilting in the breeze as a result of natural elasticity. But this morning it vibrated with uncommon vigor. As he experienced a muscle spasm under his right shoulder blade, like the fluttering of a trapped bird, Binx assured himself that Froelich was still asleep, safely anchored by his elbows and knees. This was a plausible explanation; he had good reason to believe it. And yet . . . something felt different. Even as he was slow to wake, Binx remembered how it normally felt when Froelich was sleeping. He remembered how it was *supposed* to feel.

Fully alert now, he considered his options. Gordy was due shortly with breakfast. Still, that left minutes to kill, if not longer. So on this morning, just like every other morning, Binx braced his hands against his knees and supported the ladder with his back. He tried to construe its weight not as a burden but as a comfort. Despite his suspicion that he was talking to himself, he relayed a message up the rungs:

Froelich, he said, *I've been meaning to tell you. The other day, Gordy came around with a feather he'd found. He said he didn't know what bird it belonged to, but it must be huge, this bird, since the feather was twice as long as his arm. I didn't tell him it was a frond—just an ordinary deer fern, you see? I said it was a condor feather—and he believed me! I said you'd seen them nesting in the double-rungs and that he should look out for bird poop. He hid under the wood tarp, he was so scared!*

It was a fabrication, meant to provoke a response: Gordy knew the difference between a leaf and a feather. Gordy could fix a wristwatch, play a game of chess, and even speak a little German. People only treated him like a dunce because of his bare feet and his drawl, and Gordy was disinclined to correct them. Better some kind of fool, he always said, than any kind of threat. That was all well and good, but for someone as large as Binx the connotation of being stupid was most unwelcome. Anyway, the tarp had blown away the previous summer. They'd been using damp logs ever since, knowing how the smoke must irritate Froelich, and how there was nothing he could do to stop it.

Binx wasn't delusional—he knew that no one was listening. Still, his uncle had been a constant presence since before he was born. When they were kids, Binx had made Gordy practice TAP with him, so he could someday communicate via the ladder. They'd pounded their feet on the schoolroom floor while their teacher droned on about history and math. Even after Binx grew too large for the schoolhouse and had to wait outside on the lawn, Gordy had relayed information by stomping his heels. Not long after turning sixteen, when Binx had replaced Harald under-rung, Gordy also quit school, claiming to be bored and determined to become famous. But Binx had known the truth: without his brother to provide basic services, such as cooking and cleaning, Binx wouldn't have lasted a week. The ladder was balanced in the center of the meadow, far removed from any amenities, and Binx could not avail himself beyond arms' reach.

Since there was nothing better to do, he resumed his weary banter:

What's the weather like, Froelich? I'd ask if you can see rain, but that joke never gets old, does it? Surprise—you're all wet! Hope you weren't eating! Or reading! Or sleeping! Hey, you know what else is funny? Rot. These pants are practically falling off my body. It's not so bad during summertime, but have you ever tried mending your own clothes? Try holding a piece of hair between your thumb and finger and stitching a seam—that's what it's like for me! Better yet, try having a conversation with a piece of wood.

31

By the time Gordy arrived with their breakfast, the better part of an hour had passed. "Morning, Binxy," he said, failing to acknowledge his brother's despondency. Gordy was dressed for town, from his bowler cap to his red suspenders. The only thing missing were socks and shoes.

"I hope you're hungry," he continued, "because Miss Sarah has labored under that assumption."

In his hands, Gordy was carrying a tidy parcel. When he unwrapped the linen napkin, Binx saw it contained bacon, eggs, and bread, as well as a jelly jar of lard. As was her habit, Miss Sarah had provided a triple ration: one for Gordy and two for Binx, commensurate with his size. It was a tempting sight, to say the least, and Binx's stomach rumbled again, but a fleeting detail nagged at him.

"You went all the way to Miss Sarah's farm? Why not Luther's?"

Gingerly placing the eggs on the ground, Gordy stoked the fire and grinned. "That's a good question!" he said, picking a fleck of dirt off the bacon. "I can see the early hour hasn't affected your brain. Me, I get some of my best ideas before it's even light out. A darkened sky is like thinking with your eyes closed!"

The smell of rendered lard was making it hard to concentrate. Still, Binx persisted: "You didn't answer my question."

"Didn't I? What was the question again?"

"Miss Sarah's farm. Why'd you go all the way—"

"Oh, yes! Did you know she's got a cousin visiting?

Hiram, his name is. A reporter from Philadelphia. Well, he *was* a reporter. But since he's here, and the job's back there, I can't imagine he's a reporter any more. Not that there's a shortage of stories to be found here in Oregon. Even in Boxboro—"

"No."

Pursing his lips, Gordy flipped the bacon on the skillet, hissing and flinching when it spat grease.

"Too provincial?" he said. "But what good is news, if not news of oneself? You can write about the Pope in Rome, but I'd rather read about Luther's barn—whether or not he's patched that hole. Or if the late thaw will mean hungry bears, or—"

"The answer's no, d—n it, just like last time and the time before. Don't you ever listen?"

Tipping the contents of the skillet onto two plates, Gordy tossed the bread in last to fry. "Just for conversation's sake, do you know what an article could mean for us?"

"Shame?" Binx snorted. "Embarrassment? Do you want to be the butt of every last joke, or for people to learn how Harald died?"

"Attention's not always a bad thing, you know. And not just local attention—*national* attention. Traveling dignitaries. How'd you like to meet Johnny Appleseed?"

"What I'd like to meet is my d—ned breakfast. Give it here!"

Grunting with frustration, Gordy surrendered the plate—tending to the bread, and shoveling a handful of eggs into his mouth. Binx gave his brother an

33

exasperated look as he too wolfed down his meal, nearly twice the portion allotted for Gordy. The day Johnny Appleseed stood under the ladder would be the day that Gordy met his idol.

"You're an idiot," Binx said.

"Well," Gordy mused as he gnawed on a piece of bacon, "I respectfully disagree. And I don't see why you get to decide. Shouldn't we ask Froelich?"

It was only with some difficulty that Binx managed to swallow. "We can't."

"Why not?"

"Because he's gone."

"Who's gone?"

"Uncle Froelich. He's missing."

It took a moment for this concept to sink in. "What d'you mean, *missing*?" Gordy asked, the look on his face changing from wonder to bewilderment.

"I mean missing from the ladder."

"Since when?"

"I don't know—yesterday? The day before that? I only realized it this morning."

"He's probably just ignoring you."

Normally, Binx would've agreed. Froelich's feelings could be easily hurt, and playing deaf was his favorite punishment. But today that wasn't the case.

"Not ignoring me," he said, shaking his head deliberately. "Not here."

Then Gordy did the only natural thing: he stared straight up into the sky, even though it was pointless. The ladder kept rising beyond the tallest tree, where it became lost in the leaves. On a good day, they could distinguish clear up to the four-hundred-rungs from where they were standing, but Froelich hadn't ventured lower than the hundred-rungs since they were kids.

In all of recorded history, Froelich's ladder was the fourth tallest that had ever been erected. The tallest, of course, had been Jacob's ladder—which, even if it was fictional, had still been conceived of by man, and therefore had to be counted among his many accomplishments. In truth, neither Gordy nor Binx had any idea how tall the ladder was—not precisely, anyway. Froelich claimed the Very Big Tree had never ceased to grow. *He* claimed never to have seen the top of the ladder, suggesting it might be infinite. When Binx reminded him that Harald had carved the other end, and therefore the ladder *couldn't* be infinite, Froelich had given the TAP equivalent of a shrug.

Gordy turned to face the far side of the meadow, taking in the lean-to, the wood pile, and the lonely fulcrum—shaped, to Binx's eye, like an abandoned ax head. Not finding what he was looking for there, he began to pace around the foot of the ladder, inspecting every inch of dirt.

"What're you doing?" Binx asked him.

"Checking for footprints."

"Footprints? Whose footprints?"

"Froelich's, of course! Who do you think?"

For a moment, he departed from Binx's field of vision, circling around to the far side of the ladder. When he reappeared, Binx cleared his throat.

"Let me understand this. You're searching for Froelich's footprints . . . on the ground? You think maybe he climbed down to the double-rungs, *over me*, and then walked away?"

"Also, scuff marks."

"You think maybe he climbed down while I was sleeping, then *scuffled* with someone?"

Refusing to meet Binx's eye, Gordy muttered, "Anyway, that's what I'm looking for."

"Brother," Binx said. "Quit it—there ain't any footprints. The only possibility is that he fell."

"Has he ever fallen before?"

"It only has to happen once."

"Still, where's the proof?"

"I don't need any proof! He's gone—I can feel it. Try sitting down for a minute. Take some deep breaths until you start making sense."

Grudgingly, Gordy obliged.

"He's probably just napping."

"In the middle of the day? It's too bright out."

"Well . . . what if he did fall? Where'd he land? I don't see any Froelich-shaped holes in the ground, do you?"

When Binx craned his neck to demonstrate his limited range of motion, Gordy protested, "But why now? It hasn't rained in weeks. So, what—maybe he got poached by a cloud? Shouldn't we at least check? You say Froelich's missing from the ladder—shouldn't we know for sure?"

"And how do you propose we do that?"

"Climb it ourselves, of course! Just to see!"

Binx began to shake his head. At the same time, Gordy clambered to his feet.

"No way," Binx grunted. "No, sir."

"Yes! It'll be easy!"

"Easy? Easy for you to say! You're not the one holding two people on his back—*if* Froelich is up there. Which, by the way, is against the rules, holding two people!"

"Given the situation, I think we can suspend the rules. Now, if you're not strong enough to hold us, I can get the fulcrum . . ."

"Don't be ridiculous," Binx snapped. "Of course I'm strong enough to hold you. Look, it's past noontime already—it'll be dark before you're ready to come down. And don't say you can sleep up the rungs, because you can't."

But Gordy had planted himself in front of his brother, resolute and erect. In his undershirt and suspenders, Binx thought he looked like a candy cane, and briefly considered saying so. He further considered whether they'd be having this conversation if Harald were still alive. But then he'd be the one holding the ladder, not Binx.

"You can make all the arguments you want," Gordy reasoned, "and some of them might even be right. But don't pretend like everything's normal when it's not! Sooner or later you'll want answers. Is he up there or isn't he? So how long are we going to stand around, trying to come up with a reason? Anyway, I'm not done with Hiram. If you won't ask Froelich, I will."

The wind shifted directions then, carrying with it the scent of honeysuckle. Binx's plate was empty, and the forgotten bread had since charred in the skillet. Inhaling deeply, he scratched his elbow by rubbing it against a rung. Who would suggest that things were normal? Was spending your whole life in the shadow of a ladder *normal*? With a neck like a plow horse from bearing the weight? If things were normal, they'd be throwing more wood on the fire, using the soggiest, smokiest logs they could find. More than anything, he resented that Froelich (wherever he was) would deprive him of this one small pleasure: choking their uncle on toxic fumes. Looking toward the heavens, Binx sighed.

"Three points of contact at all times," he said. Gordy clapped his hands and doffed his cap. "Be sure to climb with your legs, and not your hands. Don't think in terms of up-and-down, but—"

"—forward-and-backward. I know, I know!"

As he came around to the other side, Gordy poked his toes into the small of Binx's back.

"You okay?"

"Fine," Binx said, clutching the stiles with both hands.

"Remember how we used to practice on trees? And that one time, when I fell on you?"

"Brother?" he hissed through clenched teeth. "Less talking. More climbing."

At first, it was fairly easy to hear each other speak, but then the wind picked up, plucking their words from the air and making it necessary to communicate via TAP. Gordy had fallen out of practice, rendering his vocabulary uncharacteristically blunt.

Cold. More cold than expected.

Maybe socks would help?

Shut up.

I'm surprised there's even time for you to complain. Shouldn't you be at the top by now?

Shouldn't you shut up?

When they were younger, Harald had allowed them climb to twice his height. Binx, formerly the more adventurous of the two, had sneaked even higher, ascending past the treetops; but this was before the bloom of adolescence, when his size and weight would've betrayed him. He could recall the view from on high, like a dream he'd been snatched from. The thrill of defying gravity remained just as tantalizing.

On the lower rungs, where the spiders spun their fusty webs, the wood was more absorbent, minimizing the risk of sweaty palms. Farther up it could be dangerously slick. Each rung possessed its own identity, and Froelich had continued to decorate them all, scratching odd scripts and patterns over the years. Binx expected that Gordy would find himself distracted as he made his way higher and higher.

How's the view? Binx asked. From the double-rungs, one could see over the forest and toward the horizon. When he reached the hundred-rungs, Gordy would be awarded his first glimpse of Boxboro, more than a mile away.

I can see Miss Sarah's farm, he replied. *Do you think Froelich ever watches us?*

Binx had entertained this thought before: that Froelich must observe their daily interactions, or else be privy to their secrets, should he be intrigued. It was a disquieting idea, that some remote witness was observing everything. Even more distressing was the notion that he could, but might choose not to—that one's day-to-day existence might not warrant attention.

I couldn't say. Any signs of him yet?

Not yet. Should it move so much?

Binx could feel the resulting tremors as Gordy hooked an elbow over a rung and rapped against a stile, faithfully maintaining three points of contact. From the ground, the stiles appeared to be perfectly stationary, but up high, where Gordy was continuing his ascent, the swaying became more pronounced, with all the attendant creaks, groans, and shifts in equilibrium.

It's because you're bigger than Froelich—not to be rude. Do you think maybe you should come down?

I'm not coming down. I'm fine.

Then concentrate on climbing, Binx admonished his brother, willing him hand over hand, rung over rung, despite the frequency of the oscillations. Were Gordy to allow himself a peek (not down, of course, but *backward*), any view of the meadow would be obscured by the trees. From the hundred-rungs, the residents of Boxboro would be hard to distinguish, making the town appear to be deserted.

Gordy?

It's windy!

That's the slipstream, Binx replied, remembering what Harald had told him. *Make sure you hold on tight. How about Froelich? Can you see him?*

No. Wait! Let me ask this guy. No—he says no.

Ha, ha, very funny. Okay, let's make a deal. If you haven't found him by sunset, you should come down immediately.

Here's another deal—you put on a dress and I'll call you Binxerella. There's lots of clouds up here. I thought you said they didn't fly this low?

Binx frowned, while a shift in the breeze filled his nose with burnt toast. It had been a late thaw that spring, meaning less pollen than usual. Hungry cloud calves, separated from the herd, might've descended in search of food, but he couldn't recall anything of that nature from previous years.

It's not normal, he admitted, thinking of what Gordy had said about Froelich being poached. *How big are they? Can you see?*

Maybe if I climbed a little higher.

From where he was standing, Binx couldn't see Gordy, not even the soles of his feet. He could only imagine the series of mistakes that would ultimately lead to his fall. First, as the stiles swayed, Gordy would begin to climb on a downbeat, rather than wait for the following oscillation. The resulting momentum would cause his feet to slip, which would inspire him to rely more thoroughly on his hands and shoulders.

Gordy? Don't worry about the clouds. Make sure you're holding on.

He'd require a free hand with which to respond. Gordy's second mistake would involve releasing the rung, in order to rap on the stile. Thus, while assuming he was maintaining three points of contact, only one

41

point of contact would actually be secure. During the ladder's next oscillation, when the momentum shifted in gravity's favor, his feet would suddenly vanish from underneath him—and, just like that, he'd be dangling by one hand.

Gordy—what's happening? Why aren't you talking? The air gets thin up there. Are you dizzy? Disoriented? Don't answer that. Just grab the nearest rung and take deep breaths.

Gordy's third mistake, as dictated by the previous two, would be to rely exclusively on his upper body—not that he'd have any choice. His one hand wouldn't be strong enough to support his weight. Maybe, if he'd spent the previous month in training, the situation would be different, but the point was moot. When the ladder swayed in the opposite direction, it would casually fling him into the wide, blue sky, like a fisherman casting bait.

Gordy? Binx tapped. *Just hang on, brother. Everything is gonna be okay.*

CHAPTER 4

Gordy was plummeting through space—which, much to his relief, proved to be less harrowing than he might've expected. In fact, he'd been more afraid while still clinging to the rungs. Now that he was airborne, there were other sensations to compete for his attention: the intense cold, the rushing wind, and the view of the sunset he was uniquely afforded.

Then he was crashing through a canopy of trees, and that part was extremely painful. Once, as a boy, he'd fallen from a birch limb and landed on top of Binx, both of them sustaining minor injuries; this was similar to that experience, only far worse. Among other places, he was battered in the neck, groin, hips, ribs, spine, one knee, and also the other knee. Finally, after his body had been thoroughly pulverized, he had the good fortune to snag on a branch—landing on his stomach, with his limbs dangling over the sides.

The light was much dimmer here, now that he had departed from the stratosphere. To his right and far below, he caught a glimpse of a fast-moving river: the Columbia, he assumed. Gordy didn't recognize its shape, making him think he was miles from home. In the gloaming, the current rippled like an enormous snake. All around him, leaves rustled and boughs groaned. And then there was a *snap*, and he was falling again—only, this time, he landed on his head. Moments later, the branch that had been supporting him also came down, and Gordy was plunged into darkness.

He woke sometime later with a pain like a gong.

"What is it?" somebody was yelling. "Is we under attack?"

Coaxing one eye open, Gordy observed the glow of a campfire. Then he was being hauled to his feet, urgent hands poking and prodding him.

"Who're you?" a second voice demanded to know. "Where're you comin' from?"

There were two men, one of them fat and the other one thin, both of them dressed in rags. After they'd leaned him up against a tree, they scurried back, standing on either side of the campfire, such that their faces were only partially illuminated.

"You a moon man?" asked the fat one, jabbing a finger at him.

"Or a Irishman?" accused the other.

When Gordy attempted to speak, he found the pain

in his skull to be too overwhelming. Standing with his hands on his thighs, he raised a finger, requesting a moment.

"If you *ain't* no moon man, then who's the president of the United States?" the first one persisted.

"That's right! Or the president of Ireland!"

In an audible whisper, the fat man asked, "Nantz, what is it with you and the Irish?"

"I told you, Carmichael, I killed a Irishman at Murfreesboro—only, he wouldn't die! I tried arsenic, I tried castor beans—I even tried choking him! I swear, the whole time I had my hands 'round his neck, he was singing a dirge. It went on so long, I thought it was the Resurrection."

Gordy had already pegged the vagabonds as Confederates, but the mention of Murfreesboro cemented his guess. In his experience, their type was quick to violence. That they hadn't harmed him yet meant they were fearful; that they were fearful meant they lacked scruples. Gordy remained hunched over while simultaneously trying to compose his thoughts.

"Just before he passed," Nantz continued, "he swore he'd take revenge. Five brothers, he claimed he had, and twice as many cousins. He swore they'd hunt me down, no matter where I'd hide. So, if a person's gonna be jumping outta trees at other people, I'd like to know they ain't Irish!"

"Grant," Gordy wheezed, as soon as he was able. "The president of the United States is Ulysses S. Grant."

Making a sour face, the one called Carmichael spat

on the ground. "For now he is."

From the look of things, their campsite was only temporary. No shelter had been erected, nor had any laundry been hung out to dry. Even their campfire suggested impermanence, the logs chiefly consisting of green wood. Slumped in the shadows was a young boy. Even in the half light, it was plain to see that his lip had been split and his eye was bruised. Someone bigger and stronger had recently rendered a beating. It could've been either man. It could've been both.

"For what good reason was you up that tree?" asked Nantz.

"I was keeping lookout," Gordy explained.

"Lookout for what?"

When he refused to answer, the two men exchanged a glance.

"My goodness," Carmichael said, squatting and shaking his head, like he'd just remembered something amusing. "We ain't even introduced ourselves! You can call me Carmichael. This one here's Nantz. Sorry about grabbin' you—but when people start falling outta trees at other people, there's reason to be skittish. No hard feelings?"

Gingerly testing his shoulder, Gordy conveyed indifference.

"That's nice—we ain't looking for trouble. We're traveling north. You ever heard of Francis Myers? Richest man in all of Oregon? He's hiring English-speaking trappers. Me and Nantz is *expert* outdoorsmen."

"Experts at killing people, too," Nantz added.

"Or was," Carmichael agreed, "during the War. I'd say we was responsible for at least a dozen deaths—wouldn't you say, Nantz?"

"Union or Rebels?"

"I guess it don't matter which. There was that boy who'd lost a hand—he died in his sleep. And then the boy with *no* hands. Always thirsty—"

"But couldn't hold a cup," Nantz completed the thought.

"Then there was those boys from Tennessee—neighbors, they said, from the same holler. One died with a pillow to the face, the other from gangrene. Not that it matters now—it's all behind us. What matters is the present, or wouldn't you agree?"

"Who's he?" Gordy asked.

Carmichael dismissively waved his hand at the boy. "He's nothing," he said. "Less than nothing—when we get to the Logging Camp, we'll trade him for chaw. Now, what was you keeping lookout for?"

At the mention of the Logging Camp, the hair stood up on the back of Gordy's neck. He'd never been there before, but he was aware of its existence: a shantytown on the far side of the Cascades, owing its existence to Myers & Co. Maybe, not so long ago, a logger had gotten drunk and wandered down from the timberline. Maybe an Indian had come up from the Coast Reservation—and a missionary, too, because you couldn't hold a quorum without the Holy Ghost. These men would've required food and entertainment. Want begat labor, labor begat industry, and soon the Logging Camp was born.

47

The place was a haven for lost souls. Fathers and husbands, the missing and the presumed dead. Those who had a weakness for gambling or drink, or those with no weakness at all—nothing to goad their intractable hearts. Deep in the woods, where the continent still provided some measure of privacy, a man could ignore his past. He could live outside of history, were he so inclined, indulging in every sordid delight, or just one; could die a thousand deaths, or just one. The trees made for good company, neither inclined to gossip, nor did they encroach.

By the light of the campfire, Gordy regarded the boy. He had fine features: high cheekbones and lips in the shape of a heart. Still, he must've had iron at his core to endure such a beating. Somebody at the Logging Camp would pay a hefty price for him, presuming he made it that far.

"Lookout for *what*?" Carmichael growled.

If one thing would satisfy a man's doubt, it was greed. Slumping his shoulders, Gordy said, "Gold. And I wouldn't't've fallen, too! Except that he told me which branch to sit on. They're going to be so mad, when they get back!"

Gold: the word had a palpable effect on the two men. Though they tried to remain calm, their eyes grew wide and their ears pricked up. Pretending he didn't notice, Gordy swiped his foot against the ground.

"Who's gonna be mad?" Carmichael said.

"My boss! But *I'm* the one who should be steamed—I could've hurt myself! I said it wouldn't hold, but he never listens. If he did, they wouldn't be stumbling around in the dark like a bunch of fools!"

"Never you mind them!" Nantz yipped. "What's this about gold?"

Carmichael cut him off, focusing on Gordy with unnerving intensity. "How's that, he never listens? I bet you got some good ideas. Like what, for example?"

"I'm not supposed to say . . ."

"Listen, it's just us out here. Don't you worry about the boss man—he sure as sugar ain't worried about you! Where'd you be right now, if we hadn'ta catched you? Like you said—hurt or worse!"

"But you didn't catch me," Gordy protested, momentarily forgetting himself. "I hit the ground!"

"No, I'm pretty sure we catched you. Nantz, wouldn't you say you catched him?"

"I sure would." The skinny man nodded. "You bet I catched him."

"See? We saved your life! Which is lucky, because there's lots of ways to die in the woods—especially out here, all alone. Now, why don't you tell me about this gold?"

Gordy made sure they could see him thinking. "The far side of the river," he finally confessed. "That's where you'll find it. A prospector sold my boss the claim. They all went upstream, to where there's a ferry. Only, if he'd listened to me, they didn't have to go. I could see where it's not too deep, from way up in that tree. They could've forded the river right here!"

The Confederates reached a consensus without

having to speak a word; all that remained was to suss out the details. "You hear that, Nantz?" Carmichael purred. "Paid for the paper—means he'll have it on him."

"Means they ain't expecting a fight."

"How many'd you say they were?"

Not wanting to overdo it, Gordy ventured, "Four?"

"You hear that, Nantz? *Four*."

"And no lookout."

Hauling the impassive boy to his feet, Carmichael fixed his eyes on Gordy, declaring, "Take us there."

There wasn't any moonlight to guide them, so they made their way by the sound of the water—that and the stars above, winking down from between the trees. Beside the ache in his head, Gordy had been hobbled by the fall, and yet he still had a lighter step than his coterie. Carmichael and Nantz negotiated the underbrush like a pair of boars. If Gordy had wanted to escape, he could've. Twice they got separated, and twice he had to summon them back. But Carmichael was dragging the young boy by the arm. To part with them now would mean ill tidings for their ward, and a blight on Gordy's conscience. So instead he stuck to his original plan.

When they finally arrived at the riverbank, it was a stupefying sight, like the earth was slipping sideways. Were it not for the constellations' reflection on the water, it might've resembled an avalanche, the landscape scoured clean.

"Jesus!" whistled Nantz. "You got a way across *that*?"

"It's more shallow than it looks. Just go straight ahead."

"You first."

"Me?" Gordy squeaked. "If I'm *in* the river, I can't show you the way. I won't be able to see the path!"

"What path? I thought you said it's a straight line."

"Look, if you'd rather wait, we can go at first light . . ."

"Holy Moses," Carmichael huffed, tugging at his shirt and kicking off his shoes. "Enough talk! If we wait till morning, they'll beat us here. Get in the d—ned water, Nantz. Quit being such a crybaby!"

Thus, timidly, the two men entered the river, while Gordy and the boy remained onshore. Carmichael and Nantz walked gingerly, shoulders up around their ears and clothes held high, the starlight illuminating their pale torsos.

"Don't worry," Gordy whispered to the boy. "It won't take long."

"Are we goin' straight?" Carmichael hollered to the shore.

"Straight as an arrow," Gordy replied.

"The water's so fast!"

"What's he think?" Gordy muttered. "I can make it any slower?"

"WHAT?"

"I said, hold onto each other! For balance!"

Groping at his portly companion, Nantz insisted, "Hold onto me, Carmichael—for balance!"

Ironically, it was the slender man who brought them down. When he slipped on a rock, already sternum-deep, Nantz refused to relinquish his grip on his friend. Rather than anchor them in place, Carmichael also lost his purchase, and together they were dispatched in a matter of seconds—so fast, there was hardly time to hear them scream.

Only after they'd vanished from sight did the boy speak—his voice more tenor than baritone. "My daddy says never cross a river at night."

"Yeah?" Gordy replied. "He sounds like a smart man, your daddy."

"Nah. He says lots of things."

With dawn still hours to come, Gordy trudged back toward the Confederates' campsite, followed by his companion. When Gordy paused along the way to collect firewood, the boy stopped too, always lingering at a distance, offering neither his assistance nor his gratitude. After they got back and the fire had been fed, there was nothing to eat and little to do. The only sport was staring at each other, which Gordy expected would bore him to sleep.

"Ma runs a boarding house," the boy finally volunteered, breaking the silence. "You can eat something, if you like."

"I'd appreciate that. I'm Gordy, by the way."

"I'm Gak."

"*Gak?*"

"Something wrong with your ears?"

Gordy sighed. "No, I guess not."

"What was you doing up there really, in that tree? You ain't no lookout."

"I fell off a ladder."

"A *ladder*?" Gak snorted. "You fell off a ladder and

into a tree?"

"Yeah, well." Moving his body a little closer to the fire, Gordy laced his fingers behind his head. "Let's just say it's a really big ladder."

CHAPTER 5

In front of strangers, her siblings called her Gak. They'd found that three women invited more attention than two women and a teenage boy, so with their daddy missing and Hollis not yet big enough to lift a gunnysack, Gak played a role: minding the guests, making conversation, and otherwise impersonating the man of the house. Ma ran the enterprise, but should trouble arise, as it invariably did, it was Gak who wielded the Winchester over the mantel.

Despite his heroics at the riverside, Gordy was treated no different: Gak didn't reveal her true sex, nor did Hollis or Dolly betray her secret. Good to her word, she provided Gordy with a breakfast of steak and eggs, washed down with an inky cup of coffee. While he hacked away at his slab of meat, the children openly stared at him, kicking their feet under the kitchen table like they were treading water. Upstairs, Ma's footfalls marked her progress from room to room as she freshened the bed sheets.

"So, your uncle just lives up there," Gak stated, incredulous. "That's what you're saying?"

"That's what I'm saying," Gordy agreed, using his knife and fork like a drunken sawbones.

"How come I've never heard of this ladder before, if it's so big?"

Rubbing the back of his head and wincing, Gordy said, "You should've. You will. It's gonna be famous."

"But . . . on a ladder? He lives up there, way on the very top?"

"Everyone's gotta live somewhere."

"Sure," Gak scoffed. "And everyone's gotta eat. So what's he have for food?"

"Eggs, seeds—whatever he can find. There's a garden."

"A garden? What's he grow—squash?"

Dolly whispered something in Hollis's ear and the two of them giggled. Sometimes, just the sight of Gak in pants was enough to set them off. Quick as a whip, Gak separated them, hauling Hollis's chair away from the table such that the legs made an aggrieved sound.

"It ain't polite to tell secrets," she reprimanded her younger brother. Then, turning to her sister, "Maybe there's something you'd like to ask our guest?"

"Where's he *go*?" Dolly queried Gordy, her eyes twinkling mischievously. Dressed in a patchwork of purple and green, Dolly resembled a bird of paradise, perched

on the edge of her seat. Gak tried to recognize her garment from its previous incarnation, whether as a quilt or
a curtain, but Dolly had done an expert job of seaming,
rendering it something completely different.

"Where's he go?" Gordy echoed. "Mostly up-and-
down, depending on his needs. Only, Froelich would
say it's forward-and-backward, on account of—"

"No," Dolly interrupted him, fighting back a snicker.
"I mean, where's he *go*?"

Catching her meaning, and glancing back and forth
between the two of them (poor Hollis barely able to
keep a straight face), Gordy shook out his napkin.

"When Froelich goes," he said, "he just *goes*—and
the rest of us try to stay dry."

The children delivered the expected response: scan-
dalized delight. Hollis, in particular, was incensed,
laughing so hard that his nose whistled, which inspired
even Gak to grin. Finally, their guffaws were curbed by
a noise from upstairs: a note, or tone, inaudible to their
guest, which caused the three of them to stiffen.

"So . . . who-all else?" Gak inquired, trying without
success to paint the moment as unremarkable. Meanwhile,
Dolly and Hollis retreated into themselves, their faces going slack. "Standing under the ladder, trying not to get
pissed on? There's you, your daddy and ma—?"

"My brother Binx," Gordy informed her. "It's just the
two of us. Lotsee died while she was birthing him, and
Harald passed away two years ago."

"We had a brother who died when he was born,"
said Dolly, solemnly.

Gak waved a hand. "You're too little to recall." She herself had been Dolly's age. All she could remember were the grim details: the labor, the bloody sheets, digging a hole in the frozen ground. "Anyway, there's no reason to dwell on it. What I'd like to know is, if this uncle of yours fell off a ladder, where's he now?"

"A cloud probably poached him—they migrate toward the coastline this time of year."

"A *cloud*?"

"It must've been hungry," Gordy said, laying down his fork and knife. "Still, it takes a long time for a cloud to digest something. Froelich should be fine, so long as he can get himself down. But it raises another question, doesn't it? Where do I find him?"

Gak didn't answer immediately, uncertain of whether or not she was being teased. Dolly and Hollis looked perplexed, too—stuck between wearing a frown and a smile. If Gordy intended to be funny, he had a strange sense of humor.

Opting for sincerity, she said to him, "I'll tell you where to look—wherever your uncle landed, he probably ended up at the Logging Camp. Everybody does, sooner or later."

At this point in the conversation, Gak was preempted by her ma, who entered the room with a basketful of laundry. A short woman with chapped hands, she'd yet to speak in the presence of their guest—not in response to Gak's battered face, which she had left unexplained, nor to any of her quips. This had had a predictable effect on Gordy, who'd seemed otherwise inclined to mind his own business. Like many men before him, he'd responded to her indifference by babbling uncontrollably.

"Thanks again for the grub, miss!" he said stupidly, while at the same time trying to conceal his plate by draping a napkin over it. "Can I help you with anything? Maybe I can carry that?"

"If you're so eager to work," Gak suggested, "there's plenty to be done. You know how to dig a hole? Or shovel s—t? If you got a strong back, there's always more s—t to be shoveled. I'd say it's worth dinner and supper—wouldn't you agree, Ma?"

"Thanks, but no," Gordy quickly demurred. "It's been nice meeting you all. But, like I was saying, I've got to find my uncle."

"And like *I* was saying," Gak echoed, standing up from the table and pushing out her chair, "he's at the Logging Camp if he's anywhere at all. There's a mail jitney that stops at the Myers & Co. Store—first come, first served. It'll save you a day's journey, walking to the coast. You wouldn't mind, Ma, if I showed our guest to the store?"

Not the faintest utterance passed her ma's lips, much less a yea or a nay. Still, a curt dialogue was taking place. When Gak had returned with her face beat up, she'd been missing for three days. Dolly and Hollis hadn't asked any questions, which was unusual for them, but Ma would hold her tongue the longest. Such as it was, she now claimed the final word in their silent debate: blithely humming a hymn and exiting the dining room with the laundry on her hip.

"She don't mind," Gak grumbled, sounding unconvincing even to her own ear. Squatting between her siblings, she took a moment to address them, draping her arms around their shoulders and swiveling her head to and fro. "I gotta go now—"

"*Again?*"

"—but I want y'all to listen. Hollis—you listening? Be good to Ma, and don't cause her any grief. Dolly's in charge while I'm away. Dolly, if there's trouble you and your brother go hide till it's safe, then run for McHenry's farm. Everyone remembers which direction that is? Okay, then—gimme a big hug."

"Is the store very far?" Gordy joked, making a bid for levity, but nobody shared his humor. With her arms wrapped around them, Gak could feel the warmth of her brother and sister, and imagined she could allay all their fears. Truthfully, any assurance would be a lie. Despite the Winchester, the hymnal, and the McHenrys' farm, death could arrive at any time and take any form: pestilence in the water or a lecherous neighbor. Life was a promise made to be broken, another hole dug in the frozen ground. None of them was really safe.

Outside, the day had become muggy, midges suspended in the air like dust motes. The road they were taking (a path frequented by homesteaders, and not unfamiliar to animal tracks) was narrow and shrouded, such that Gak could reach out and touch the trees on either side. She would've been content to walk in silence. Indeed, she might've preferred it, only Gordy seemed beset by guilt.

Stepping over a branch, he commented, "I'm sure they'll be fine."

"Who?"

"Your brother and sister—I'm sure they'll be safe."

"Safe from what?"

"Carmichael and Nantz," he promptly replied—because, apparently, the Confederates were his only context for danger.

"*Those* goons?" Gak laughed. "I'm more afeared of bee stings, if I wanted a fright. D'you know how many Rebels we've hosted, since the war between the states? Good Lord, it's been one after the other, on their way up to Canada. I tell 'em, if you hate Negroes so much, why not stay here? We've got exclusionary laws! And nooses, they say, and circuit judges. Thanks, but no thanks. Anyway, those two aren't worth losing sleep over."

Skipping over a divot in the road, she slapped at a low-hanging limb, provoking a claque of birds to take flight. Gordy observed this feat with bald skepticism.

"Oh, no?" he said. "Weren't they the ones who bruised your face? I wouldn't think too generously of whoever did it."

Delicately probing the flesh around her eye, Gak scowled. "Yeah, well . . . maybe so. But the joke's on them, ain't it? Good luck finding the Logging Camp without my help—if they do float ashore, which I doubt they will."

Abruptly, Gordy stopped walking.

"You *wanted* to go to the Logging Camp?"

"Sure I do!" Gak declared. "That's where I was going the whole time. It's safer traveling in twos and threes—though I might've picked better company. What, you thought they nabbed me?"

"I might've been informed," Gordy grumbled. When Gak failed to provide a timely response, he said it again, and louder. "I might've been informed you weren't their captive. I might've known that, before sticking my neck out for you."

Gak's first instinct was to deliver a retort: if breakfast hadn't been reward enough, he should've picked up a shovel! But, for once, she thought twice. So far, Gordy had done right by her. He'd kept his word, as well as keeping his hands to himself. If Gak were going to depend on him, she could start by being honest.

"Okay," she said, "look"—rubbing her nose and scowling—"I'm sorry if you're mad. And I'm sorry you didn't know any better. But I'm glad for what you did! You're right—those two goons did a number on me, all for making a joke. I *thought* I needed their help. Daddy traveled north in springtime, looking for work, and we haven't seen him since."

She could see the revelations striking Gordy, one after another: Ma being a California widow; the necessity of taking on boarders. While they were standing there, a particularly fat cloud moved in front of the sun and the light shifted from ocher to violet. This partial eclipse was followed by a thunderclap, so loud its reverberations spilled pollen on the breeze. They waited for the storm to come, but it never did—just the smell of rain, and electricity in the air.

"He said he'd try Fort Vancouver," Gak continued.

"But every time he leaves, I find him back at the Logging Camp. You ever been there before?"

"To the Logging Camp?" With an embarrassed smile, Gordy confessed, "I've never been anywhere but Boxboro."

"Well, I've been there lots of times. *Too* many times. Lemme show you the way. It's the least I can do, after the help you gave me."

As Gordy mulled this idea, Gak tried to appear ambivalent, even when he said, "Sure—why not."

Resuming their march, Gak observed, "That was a pretty nifty trick you pulled." She could hear the relief in her voice, even if Gordy couldn't.

"What was?"

"Getting the Rebels to cross the river like that."

"Yeah, well—it wouldn't've been so nifty if they'd known how to swim."

"Say, you *ain't* an Irishman . . . are you?"

Gordy gave her a sideways glance. "What do you think?"

"Don't matter to me," Gak allowed with a shrug. "Like you said, everyone's gotta live someplace."

At the intersection of a wider road, the Myers & Co. Store came into view. The façade was identical to the McMinnville location, which Gak had visited the previous summer: same porch, same rocking chairs, even the same shade of green they'd painted the trim. She'd never seen anything so faithfully recreated—including the flag at the county clerk's office, which had been hand-stitched by the clerk's wife after a trip to Baltimore.

Tugging on the door and sounding the chime, Gak noticed Gordy still lingering on the stairs.

"You coming in?"

Looking up and down the road, he motioned to an empty chair. "I think it's best I wait. I don't want to miss it."

"You couldn't miss the mail jitney if you tried—not unless you've got cotton in your ears. Besides, we're going on a trip. We need provisions!"

"Provisions? I haven't got any money. Do you?"

"I got better," she replied happily, ushering him through the door. "Store credit!"

Inside, the air was cool. Gak nodded at the counterman, who glanced up from his ledger.

"You gotta have shoes," he said to Gordy, pointing at his bare feet. "I can't be of service if you don't have any shoes."

"Oh, hush now, Horace," Gak scoffed. "Since when is that a rule?"

Undaunted, she continued down the aisles, Gordy trailing. Together they inspected the shelves' contents: Mason jars, candles, and spools of twine. There were various foodstuffs by the front, but Gak was looking for one item in particular: apricots, which were only in season for a short time and always stored in a cool, dark place.

But when they came to the appropriate corner, the barrel was empty. All she found was a display of stepladders, neatly folded and stacked against the wall.

"Funny thing," Gordy said, tilting his head to one side.

"What's that?"

Stepping closer, he ran his fingers along the moving parts—the planes and hinged stiles. "Makes me homesick, is all. Still, it's got about as much in common with Froelich's ladder as the business side of an oar."

"A ladder's a ladder," Gak replied, plunging her torso into the barrel and kicking her trousers in the air.

"Not so! There's cat ladders and orchard ladders, roof ladders and trestle ladders. They can be made from rope or hemp. Did you know, the second tallest ladder in history was made of gold?"

Failing to find any apricots at the bottom, Gak climbed out of the barrel. "You don't say," she muttered, elbowing past him.

But try as she might to convey disinterest, Gordy proceeded to tell her the entire story—even following Gak up and down the aisles while she made her way back to the counter:

"The pharaoh's wife commissioned it, after he died. See, in Egypt, it was custom to be buried with your slaves. But the pharaoh's wife wanted to send more. She worried he wouldn't have enough, not to last for all eternity, except she didn't want to disturb his tomb—so she had a golden ladder smelted, and told those slaves to get climbing!"

At the front of the store, with her palms splayed on the counter, Gak considered her options: pickled eggs, rock candy, and a vast assortment of jerky—deer jerky, turkey jerky, even salmon jerky. At her direction, the counterman marked his place in the ledger and shook out a paper sack.

"At dawn," Gordy said, "the slaves started to climb. But as the day went on, the ladder turned hotter and hotter. By afternoon, the rungs were too hot to hold. When the first hundred slaves fell to their deaths, they all turned to locusts. When the second hundred fell, they all turned to frogs. The third hundred turned to blowflies—until there was so many plagues visited on the land of Egypt that the pharaoh's wife was stoned to death."

"Say, Horace," Gak inquired. "Where's the apricots? I checked in back, but I couldn't find any."

"Late thaw this year—try again in a couple of weeks." With a smirk and a glance at her companion, the counterman added, "Is that all that you need, Gabrielle?"

"*Gabrielle?*" Gordy blurted out. "You're a girl?"

This was entirely the problem with pretending to be a boy: one innocent remark could ruin the illusion. After she'd been revealed there was no way to talk herself out of it. Gordy would be mad, she knew; nobody liked to be fooled. But at least he wasn't violent (or didn't seem to be). If Carmichael and Nantz had learned her secret, she would've been raped and murdered for sure.

"Oh, is that a secret?" the counterman said. "Since when?"

"Shut up," she snapped at him. "Anyway, so what? What's Gordy short for—*Gordon?*"

"Yeah, but that's different. I just thought—"

"Hollis can't say Gaby—he can't pronounce it—so he says Gak instead. There's your mystery. If you're too dumb to see what's in front of you, it ain't my fault. Anything else I can explain for you, *Gordon*?"

"No, I—"

"Then quit your yapping. Maybe if you stopped talking long enough, you'd know the mail jitney's here."

From outside, they could hear a rattle and whinny, wafting on the wing of a rank odor. While the gears continued to turn in Gordy's head, Gak gathered up her food.

"Charge it to my account, Horace. And you can wipe that d—ned silly grin off your face."

With that, Gak was out the door. As her vision readjusted from the dark interior, she spotted the amorphous shape of a horse and carriage. The peculiarities of the driver as he dismounted from the wagon, presumably with a bundle of letters in hand, were only just beginning to emerge.

"You there!" she barked at him, striding right up. "I'm on my way to the coast. Take me there?"

"You, or your friend too?"

Behind her, Gordy had stooped to retrieve a piece of jerky that she'd accidentally dropped. Gak barely afforded him a glance.

"Who says he's my friend? Are we holding hands? Are we laughing and smiling and telling secrets? Now, can I get a ride with you or not?"

The driver scratched his chin. Blinking in the bright sunlight, Gak was afforded a better perspective of the man: broad across the shoulders, with close-set eyes.

Not someone she'd normally care to provoke.

But, contrary to her expectations, he shrugged his assent. "Fine with me, I guess. You can ride in back. Just don't touch the mail, is all."

Still frowning, he plodded past them—throwing a quizzical look at Gordy and the piece of jerky in his hand before stepping inside.

"Like I'd want to sit with you," Gak grumbled. "Oh, you mean I can't? Well, boo-hoo-hoo."

Climbing onto the back of the wagon, she girded herself for what was to come. Gordy was still bound for the coast—he'd still require a ride. Maybe he'd ignore her. Most likely he'd tease her, but that would soon lose its sport. What was crucial was that he not mention her sex to the driver, but how could she be assured of that? Even to ask him now would risk being overheard. Gak squirmed as he approached, knowing herself to be completely exposed.

Gordy stopped on the dirt track. "There's something I mean to get off my chest," he said. "If I don't own up to it, I believe I'll regret it." Waiting for Gak to catch his eye, he waved the piece of jerky in her face. "I don't know if this is salmon or maybe something I stepped in, but I'm gonna eat it. I'm gonna eat it, and it's gonna taste better than your ma's breakfast. So what do you say about that?"

The horse snorted and pawed at the ground. For her part, Gak stared up at the sky. How to translate this attempt at humor? Clearly, he meant to put her at ease, but why? To what purpose? Far overhead, the clouds cast their shadows upon the land, like pools of indeterminate depth.

"I lied to you," she said.

"You don't need to apologize."

"Who's apologizing?" Gak snorted. "I'm just owning what I did."

"Still, you didn't lie—you skipped the truth. Is there anything else you might've skipped?"

Taking a deep breath, she resolved herself to act in good faith. "Yeah," she said. "That ain't salmon jerky, it's deer. And you're right—the way Ma cooks, it's like she's mad at the food. Still, I hope you eat it, and I hope it tastes like s—t."

CHAPTER 6

The crashing of the waves was faint from Josie's tower, though the odor of seaweed was rank. Assuming that first light wouldn't be long, she swung her legs off the bed and blindly felt for her shoes. She was still wearing her clothes from the night before, saving her the effort of dressing in the dark. She even had an extra shawl, which she now deemed unnecessary. There were no provisions to pack, no correspondence to be made. As soon as her laces were tied, she proceeded with resolve.

She accessed the stairwell quickly and quietly. Feeling her way along the rough-hewn wall, Josie descended the irregular turret steps. If pitch darkness could be improved upon, here it was utterly black, save for the faint outline of a doorway below her. On the other side of that border Lieutenant Harrison would be standing sentry. If Josie were lucky, he'd be sleeping at his post; if not, she was duly prepared to charm him.

Upon stepping outside, she was able to distinguish her arms and legs—and there too was Lieutenant Harrison, leaning against the wall with a woolen blanket around his shoulders. If he hadn't been asleep, he wasn't fully awake either, coquettishly blinking his eyes.

"Good morning, Miss Josephine," he yawned. "You're up early."

Josie smiled at his obtuseness. A quick look around confirmed there was no one else present; the parade ground was empty, and the postern gate closed.

"Yes," she said, "I was hoping for a short walk."

Like a dog catching a scent, the lieutenant was immediately keen to her, rousing himself to a more attentive posture.

"A walk, you said? I'm not so sure about that. Did you ask Mr. Myers? Maybe if wc tell the Sergeant Major first—"

"Harrison," Josie cut him off, "what age are you?"

Having already conceived of such a moment, she now placed her hand on his chest. Not on his face, which would've been too intimate, but not his shoulder, either, which could've been dismissive. His chest, Josie had decided, would strike the perfect balance between familiar and flirtatious.

Her touch achieved the desired effect. Blanching, he stuttered, "What age? Seventeen."

"Seventeen," Josie repeated. "I am nineteen. Doesn't that strike you as rather old for a nanny?"

When she gave him her most winning smile, the young lieutenant returned the favor—possibly blushing, even, though it was difficult to say in the feeble light. With gray dawn fast approaching, it wouldn't be long before the whole of Fort Brogue started to wake. The smile sagged a little on Josie's face, but she kept her eyes trained on his.

"It's just a walk," she murmured, removing her hand from Harrison's chest. "I shouldn't think I require anyone's permission—certainly not at this hour."

"Maybe I can come with you?" he hopefully suggested.

"And leave your post? I wouldn't want you to be derelict. You stay here—I won't be gone for long."

Turning toward the postern gate, Josie assumed a pace of casual self-assurance. One more guard stood between her and freedom. For obvious reasons, the fort was kept secured during the night; the gate would have to be opened manually. But much could be accomplished on the suggestion of authority. It was amazing how the dynamics of momentum applied to a body even so large as the Army.

"Where are you going?"

It was Harrison again. Freezing in her tracks, Josie's mind raced. She couldn't tell him the truth: he'd never let her go if she answered him honestly. And what if he were interrogated in her absence? She wouldn't put it past her Uncle Francis. Whatever her answer, the young lieutenant was all but certain to repeat it.

"I'm going for a lunt," she said, delivering the words nonchalantly.

"A what?"

"Gone lunting. Don't you say that in America? Walking while smoking a pipe. But you mustn't tell—my uncle would never let me hear the end of it."

Had Harrison asked her any more questions, or made further excuse to tarry, she might as well have crawled back to bed. The fort would've awoken; she would've been foiled. But instead he replied with characteristic insight, "I thought you said hunting! It rhymes."

With a grin, Josie replied, "Yes, it does, doesn't it?" And that was the end of that. Striding with newfound purpose, she found it twice as easy to convince the next guard.

Through the postern gate, Josie followed a steep and narrow path between the scrub grass and succulent plants, zigzagging her way down the bluff until she'd finally reached the beach below. Here, the smell of brine became practically overwhelming. Hugging her arms across her chest, she turned her face to the breeze. With her eyes closed, the Pacific Ocean sounded like . . . like the intersection of Bridge and High Streets on a winter's eve, distempered draft animals and even more distempered cabbies. Long ago, her friend Mae had taught her how to spot a tourist. Somebody from Edinburgh would stand off the curb, Mae had said, while the tourists would abide by the rules. Peeking one eye open, Josie found the actual view to be less inspiring. Nothing to evoke home, save for the palette: gray dunes and gray sky. Gray America.

Ahead, she spotted a piece of driftwood. Gnarled and half-buried, it looked to be the size of a settee. Fixing that landmark as her intended destination, Josie teeter-tottered across the uneven dunes until she was able to sit down and remove her shoes and stockings. It was no warmer now than it had been before, even as the dawn heralded a new day. The sand was unpleasant to the touch—the landscape, now that the fort was safely behind her, not so vastly improved.

Who *wouldn't* want to visit this land of splendor, this veritable Garden of Eden? Where the possibilities were only limited by one's own imagination? That's what Josie had told herself, anyway. Like a girl who'd been conspicuously absent for nine months, she'd excised herself from her previous life. But that wasn't her, a girl to inspire rumors. What could be further from the truth? Still, her da had assured her when she'd left, "Stay here, and you'll become your mum—not that we don't give thanks every day. Even so, nothing can change without change." Truly, standing on the quay, it had been difficult to say who was convincing whom.

Mae might've affected Josie's decision to emigrate, had she been present—but, of course, Mae had stayed away. Even Josie's da might've had a change of heart, had it not been his own brother taking receipt of her. Recalling this arrangement, Josie looked back the way she'd come. She'd always feared her mum's temper, and with good reason, but she'd not yet tested Uncle

Francis's. It was best to keep moving.

The previous night's encounter with her uncle continued to vex her. Indeed, here she was, marching into the wilderness with only half a notion of where she was going! If she hadn't been expecting Uncle Francis at that late hour, it wasn't because the two of them were estranged. In fact, they spent the majority of their days together—visiting far-flung locations of his Myers & Co. stores, discussing the strengths and weaknesses of his distributors, anything that might broaden Josie's understanding of the business. It had been clear to her for some time that she was being groomed for management, an offer that she was slow to accept. But if she'd already been pining for home, his handling of the promotion had hastened her decision.

Uncle Francis had knocked shortly after dinner—a quick, decisive rap, impossible to mistake for anyone else. When she'd called her assent through the heavy wood door, he'd entered with his eyes downcast, lest he intrude on an intimate moment.

"Good evening, Josie," he'd said, not looking up. "Is this a good time?"

She'd been reading her Virgil—in particular, the third book of the *Aeneid*. "I suppose it depends," she'd remarked, saving her place with her thumb. "A good time for what?"

He'd smiled, braving a glance. Fully entering the room, he'd crossed to the end table that substituted for a writing desk.

"Tomorrow I'll be meeting with the circuit judge.

Harper is his name, an insufferable prig. You have to wonder whether it's the chicken or egg with these people—whether they become arseholes after taking power, or if being an arsehole had everything to do with it."

"Funny observation, coming from you," Josie had commented. She'd flashed a grin to soften the blow, but caught a flicker of something in Uncle Francis's eyes. It was the same look he'd give when assessing a potential rival. In the future, she'd thought, it might be wise to hold her tongue.

"Yes, I suppose so," he'd allowed. "Anyhow, talking to Harper is only a formality. My lawyer assures me we're in the right. The Naturalization Act gives the rights of citizenship to children, and all the legal protections afforded therein."

A gust of damp air had blown up the stairway and through the cell, causing Josie to shiver under her blanket.

"That's good news," she'd said while covering her shoulders. "Only, I didn't know you were expecting?"

She'd watched the corners of his lips twitch, that malevolent flicker animating his eyes. "Oh, aye," he'd grunted, steering past her joke to arrive at one of his own. "A nine-stone, bouncing baby girl."

Josie had failed to understand, staring at him with flagging patience. Finally, Uncle Francis had rolled his eyes. "You!" he'd practically shouted. "You, you daft girl—I'm adopting *you!*"

Wherever this idea had originated, that Uncle Francis was going to adopt her, it had been news to Josie. Had her parents been informed? Had it been their idea—a way to divest themselves of her, once and for all? And didn't she have a say in the matter? One didn't choose one's own parents, or so they said, but there came an age when that no longer applied.

Josie had possessed so many questions, it had been impossible to speak. Who knew what Uncle Francis had read into her silence? Most likely, a validation. Nodding his head once, he'd wordlessly adjusted some pages on her desk, arranging them into a neat little pile. Then he'd strolled toward the door, contemplatively tucking his chin toward his chest.

"You know," he'd said, standing at the top of the stairs, "I always imagined myself having a son—someone to manage the business, when I tire of chasing every last cent. But you can do well, Josie, of that I have no doubt. If I must have a daughter, I'd want it to be you."

And thus the final indignity. Not long after Uncle Francis had left, shutting the turret door behind him, Josie had made up her mind to return to Scotland. She didn't know how such a feat could be accomplished, especially without her uncle's help; he controlled the military, and anyone else she'd encounter in town. But one thing had been abundantly clear: time was of the essence. In the morning, she'd resolved, she would search for assistance, and may fortune smile on the woman who helps herself.

The tide was now fully out. At least the beach seemed broader than it had before. Walking with her shoes and stockings in hand, Josie tried her best to ignore the continent to her left. To her right, massive boulders littered

the shallows, as grand and arresting as any Gothic ca-
thedral. While there was no one to disturb her, and with
Fort Brogue only a distant concern, she was better able
to appreciate the scenery: the wending arc of the coastline, crudely formed by time and erosion. Not so when
she ventured into town, where everything was so gar-
ishly new, like the glue hadn't dried yet.

Somebody else might've found Oregon appealing;
to Josie, it was depressing. What else could she call it?
No building was taller than a single story, or more dura-
ble than plywood. Most homes didn't even have a cellar,
either for lack of foresight, or not enough people to dig
a proper hole. Towns were named according to whimsy
(Cake, Rainbow, Merlin) or, worse yet, borrowed their
identities from existing locales (Glasgow, Denmark,
Rome). Finally, and most irksome, there wasn't any *money*. A person was as likely to pay in Confederate dollars
as he was to offer an I.O.U. It only confirmed the dogma,
which they flouted at every opportunity: *If it doesn't ex-
ist, we shall create it; if it isn't real, we will pretend.*

Of course Uncle Francis would thrive in this envi-
ronment. What might've slowed his ascent in Edinburgh
(unorthodox work habits and an aversion to hierarchy),
here were genuine assets. Recognizing a commercial
void, he'd been quick to fill it—because what was the
true nature of America, if not a great, sucking hole? The
people of Oregon required lumber that Myers & Co.
was able to provide. From the timberline to the sawmill,
from transportation to distribution, Francis hadn't left a
red cent on the table. In Scotland, his business acumen

might've been dismissed as greedy. Here, it was industry, plain and simple.

Consequently, who but Uncle Francis would build a fort, then invite the United States Army to live in it? (Indeed, who could conceive of a cheekier name than Fort Brogue?) By refusing to accept rent, he'd earned the military's fealty, thereby ensuring his own safety in the event that the Coast Reservation overflowed or that the Logging Camp erupted with violence. Most days, one couldn't distinguish the Army from his own private militia . . . especially if one happened to be a young woman, gone for a lunt, absent the approval of her legal guardian.

Looking back, she couldn't even see Fort Brogue, just an impenetrable bank of fog where her window used to be. When Uncle Francis had designed the fortifications, he'd drawn inspiration from Edinburgh Castle, incorporating a barracks, great hall, and infirmary, with parade grounds protected by a high wall. Unlike its predecessor, though, Fort Brogue had been made entirely from wood. The smell of pine, while lovely, pervaded everything. Josie couldn't go to sleep at night without imagining herself on a pile of tinder.

Eager to dispel the notion, she shook her head—freeing her long, red curls, made more irascible by the bawdy sea air. With a bark of laughter, Josie twirled. But there was no one to laugh with her, and the wind whisked her exaltation down the beach.

In the weeks before she'd left for America (indeed, before she'd even devised her plan), she'd grown accustomed to loneliness. Long walks had been a good way to clear her head. Also, she'd been able to peep through people's windows, and to imagine lives more tolerable than her own.

On one such evening, as she'd been aimlessly wandering, she'd witnessed a circus troupe passing through town, departing from Waverly Station. Elephants, trunk to tail, had lumbered behind Roman gymnasts. A strongman had carried a babe in his arms. This procession of outcasts had looked so much like a parade that Josie had naturally fallen in step.

She hadn't been the only bystander. Two boys, neither of them old enough to earn a wage, had also kept pace with the performers. They'd been the nasty sort, goading each other and tossing peanuts. Their preferred target had been a trained baboon—not the wisest of choices, given the species' propensity for violence. Perhaps the hat and leash had made it seem more tame, or that it was accompanied by a clown. Regardless, what right did they have to taunt the poor creature, stamping their feet and clapping their hands?

Josie had half expected a gruesome end. And why not? Should the baboon have elected to maul the boys, so much the better. What she hadn't been expecting was for the clown to intervene. Wearing a purple wig, prosthetic nose, and oversized shoes, he'd appeared indistinguishable from his coterie—unremarkable, in that he'd looked clownish. Neither he nor the baboon had acknowledged the hecklers. But quite without warning the clown had stopped and had removed all of his clothes. He'd done so quickly and methodically—and for every article of clothing that he'd taken off, the baboon had promptly put one on, from the clown's polka-dotted blouse to his billowy trousers. Once he'd shed everything but his undergarments (dishwater gray and not the least bit hilarious), they'd passed the leash between them, now looped around the clown's neck and held by the baboon.

What had it all meant? That man was no better or worse than beast? That roles could be reversed, whether master and subject or tormentor and victim? Regardless, it had stopped the two boys cold. Josie had also been affected. As the clown had trotted to his place in line (not a svelte man, his belly had jiggled and his feet had slapped against the pavement), the procession had continued on either side of her, parting and then seamlessly merging, until she'd been left all alone on the darkened road. Even the two boys had had the wherewithal to go home, while Josie had just stood there, her mouth agape.

Ever since her rift with Mae, she'd felt miserable, undeniably so. Whether at home or at work, she'd suffered from a dull, aching pain, like her body had been bruised on the inside. In order to console herself, she'd tried to pretend that their spat was only temporary—that, sooner or later, Mae was bound to reward Josie's patience. But now she'd been made to see: if a clown could demonstrate empathy for a monkey, surely *she* deserved better. Moving to America, if not the best or only remedy, had been the most expedient. All it had required was a letter to Uncle Francis, and here she was.

Coming upon another piece of driftwood, she

stopped for a brief rest. Ahead, there were two choices available to her. She could continue down the beach until she reached the Coast Reservation, or she could venture inland, in search of the Logging Camp. Neither prospect seemed more appealing than the next. The former was a home to Siletz Indians, without the means or Christian charity to help her; the latter had been described to Josie in the bleakest of terms. Still, if it were a champion she sought, whether a fellow runaway or sympathetic countryman, she was most likely to find him at the camp.

Dangling her shoes from one arm, she kneaded her toes in the sand. The day was advancing; soon the alarm would sound. Taking advantage of the lull, and with guarded optimism, Josie ventured forth, determined to find her own way home.

CHAPTER 7

Riding on the back of the mail jitney, Gak produced a drawstring pouch. She'd *picked up* smoking while her daddy was away—a sociable habit among the guests, and something to do with her hands. Despite the uneven ride and satchel of letters she was sitting on (which caused her to slide back and forth with the topography), she still managed to pinch a wad of tobacco and roll herself a tidy cigarette. She struck a match against her shoe, took a drag, and flicked the spent red-tip into the road.

"Let me ask you something," she said. "This uncle of yours who lives on a ladder—the ladder so tall, a person can fall off it and land in a tree? Where's he sleep?"

When Gak offered him her cigarette, Gordy took a polite puff, gasp-talking, "Up the rungs, of course."

"You mean he just holds on? Because I tried sleeping

in a tree once. I nearly broke my a—!"

"See?" Gordy said, becoming animated. "You want to learn more, right? You're intrigued? People hear about a giant ladder, they got questions!"

"Are you kidding me?" Gak guffawed. "I've got a million! Like, what's your uncle eat? What's he wearing? Is he naked up there? I mean, completely naked? Is the ladder straight up and down, or is it tilted? How much of a tilt? Is it like—"

Holding her wrist steady, Gak moved her hand back and forth, alternating the plane of her palm between vertical and horizontal.

"No," Gordy corrected her, "it's more like this—" holding his own hand at a diagonal.

"What's it leaning against, then—a tree? What if the tree gets hit by lightning? Is it an A-frame? The ladder, I mean. Because, if it's an A-frame, what if somebody climbed up the other side? What if the ladder got struck by lightning? What if—"

"It's not an A-frame," he interrupted, and continued to speak before she could unleash another barrage. "It's not leaning against a tree, either. My brother, Binx, is holding it up—it's angled against his back. The ladder's heavy, like you'd expect, but he's the size of a baby bear. That's the story I'd have them write—big ladder, big guy, big heart. Not the family history, I mean. About Froelich, sure, but nothing about how Harald died."

For a brief interlude, Gak was preoccupied by this information, if not a little confused. Gordy appeared to luxuriate in the silence, closing his eyes against the tobacco smoke and rocking with the wagon.

"But what if he's not up there?" she finally proposed. "Your uncle?"

"Of course he isn't there—I told you that already."

"But what if he never was?"

Opening his eyes, Gordy sat up a little straighter. The vacant look on his face suggested he'd never entertained the question before. "You say he's been up there your whole lives," Gak continued, unable to contain her smile. "But how do you know? Has anybody ever seen him? Have you?"

"No," Gordy sputtered, "I haven't seen him. Have you seen the Queen of England? Does that mean she ain't real? Of course he's up there—sure he is. If he isn't up there, then why'd we have the ladder?"

"I don't know—to reach stuff? Lots of people have ladders."

"Don't be idiotic. Anyway, is your daddy any less real, just because—"

Immediately, Gak could feel her ears turning a fiery red. In less time than it took to expel the smoke from her lungs, a rash had spread across her entire body, starting south of her collar and spreading to the tips of her ears. Flicking her cigarette past Gordy's face, she growled, "What're you trying to say?"

"Nothing! What I meant is—"

"I know what you meant, you horse's a—. I want to hear you say it."

When Gordy failed to respond (prudently electing to keep his mouth shut), she stuck her hand into the mail satchel and started digging around. Angrily producing a fistful of letters, Gak discarded one, two, three envelopes, before identifying a missive that suited her needs.

"My daddy's real," she sneered. "Believe me, there ain't nothing pretend about Gaylord. His belt's real, his hands are real. S—t, even his moods are real, and they can change with the wind. He's just missing, is all—same as these. Each of these is a person who's gone away. Here's one from Colorado. That's real, ain't it—the Territory of Colorado? Or is the person who wrote it just a figment of my imagination?"

"Hey!" Gordy exclaimed. "You can't do that!"

"Can't do what—*read*? Why, because I got dirt under my nails?"

"No," he admonished her, glancing at the driver and lowering his voice. "Can't touch the mail. It's private property!"

Gak took another handful of letters and defiantly tossed them in the road. "What, you don't like it when I do this? I'll tell you what I don't like—you saying what I can and can't think! It's bad enough I've got to find the bastard and bring him home. You act like it's pretend? Like I *want* to leave my brother and sister behind? Because, trust me, if I could change my daddy into something he ain't, the first thing I'd do—"

But she was unable to finish the thought; with a lurch, the mail jitney shuddered to a halt. Failing to anticipate the shift in momentum, Gak was bowled over, dislodging the mail satchel from underneath her and dumping its contents into the road.

"Now you've done it," Gordy hissed.

The driver had already dismounted from the carriage, hopping down and circling to the rear. In his hands, he was throttling his leather-knit whip, his shoulders bunched. Before he even addressed them, Gak had followed his eyes down the length of the road, to where the letters trailed around the bend.

"D—n it," he cursed. "I told you not to touch 'em. Nobody ever listens."

As he began to unfurl his whip, Gordy also leapt down from the wagon. It was only with some difficulty that Gak, still sprawled upon a bed of letters, was able to rouse herself and join him.

"Sure you did," Gordy equivocated. "I remember you saying so—and I couldn't be more sorry if I tried."

"Now I've got to hurt you."

"What?" Gak said. "The heck you do!"

But the man only rolled up his sleeves, narrowing his too-close eyes in concentration. "It's the only way to learn you."

"Friend, I respectfully disagree." Licking his lips, Gordy waited for the driver to face him. "If you want to teach us a lesson, then make us fix our mistake. Otherwise, who's gonna collect all this mail—you? That doesn't seem right, does it? Make my friend here clean it up. She's been dropping parcels ever since the Myers & Co. Store—"

"Hey!"

"—and I'm sure she'd like to make amends. After that, we can go by foot the rest of the way. Okay? It's not a lesson we'll soon forget. And a lesson learned is—"

"Wait," the driver scowled, turning to Gak. "You're saying that's a *girl*?"

In that moment, everything changed. Gordy's thoughtless slip of the tongue had skewed the dynamic. It was now altogether less likely that Gak would be whipped, punishment only meted out to a boy. And yet, the potential for harm had become even greater. In revealing her gender, Gordy had also revealed Gak's weakness.

"Of course I'm a girl!" she snapped, trying to maintain her rugged demeanor. "What, you never seen one before?"

But the driver didn't answer her. Instead, he was openly leering at her chest.

"All right," he said. "How about this, then—I get a turn with her, and we can call it even?"

Sneaking a glance at Gak, Gordy cleared his throat. "Say again, friend?"

"We both call it even—no harm done for the mess you made. And I get a minute to rut."

"The heck you do," Gak snorted, turning to leave; careful not to stumble or panic, nor waiting to hear Gordy's response.

Unfortunately, in turning to her left, she walked directly into the driver's fist. His right hook collided with her cheekbone and rattled her brain inside her skull. The next thing she knew, she was horizontal on the dirt track, pinholes of light flickering in her vision.

"What's it gonna be?" the driver said to Gordy. "I

don't *need* permission. I'm just being decent, since she's your freight."

Gak spat out a surprising amount of blood. She couldn't run: even if she were able to keep her balance, her thoughts would be too muddy to navigate. She could cause the driver some damage if he came close enough, gouging out an eye or gnawing on an ear, though it might worsen her situation. Gordy stood a chance, she thought, while attempting to raise herself on hands and knees. She doubted he was big enough or strong enough to stop the driver, but he was decent enough to try.

So it pained her when he said, "Me first, then. Like you said, she's my freight."

There came a dreadful noise, like an animal suffering under a heavy yoke, which Gak knew to be her doing. She started to crawl, even while a tiny voice urged her to hush now, be still.

"You first?" the driver echoed. She couldn't bear to listen to their deliberation. She wished she could plug her ears, or turn herself into stone.

"No, you're right—you. I don't like to be watched."

"Me?"

"Yeah, you," Gordy sighed. "You first, then me."

A foot against her backside tipped her over. Hiding her face in her elbow, Gak attempted to block out the sun.

"Wait—no. Me."

"Me?" the driver roared, turning halfway around. In silhouette, he was clumsily fumbling with his pants.

"Make up your d—ned mind!"

"No, you're right, you," Gordy said, bobbing his head and taking a step in retreat. "I'm sorry. You go right ahead. I'll just pick up some mail, why don't I?"

"Do or don't," the driver growled, "I hardly care. But shut your mouth for a d—ned minute."

In three brisk strides the brute was towering over her. Gak kicked her feet, but the driver was too strong, catching her by the ankle and giving a tug. As he flopped down on top of her, he buried a punch in her gut. All her breath departed at once—Gak reduced to sobbing and gagging, while the driver maneuvered his pants down around his hips. He snaked his fingers under her waist, their skin touching with an electric jolt.

Suddenly he pitched to his right. Even then, she continued to struggle—digging her fingers into the earth and pawing, as the road lacerated her palms. There was Gordy, holding a stick. Not a stick—a log, big enough to start a fire. He stood astride the driver and continued to bludgeon the man's head, each blow producing a hollow *thump*. Finally a shudder passed through the driver's legs and he lay perfectly still.

Gordy dropped to his knees and faced Gak, but she doubted that he saw her. His eyes were wide, his gaze turned inward, and the tears he wept mixed freely with the dirt.

CHAPTER 8

Far above them, someone was watching. Or, if not watching, in a position to observe.

What *had* happened to Froelich during the day of his disappearance, that he would've vanished into thin air? Nothing as drastic as Gordy's original notion—no scuffle at the hands of an angry mob, nor any Froelich-shaped holes in the ground. On the morning he'd gone missing, Froelich had awoken before dawn with a splitting headache. As a rule, he was constantly under the weather, which made sense, considering he was constantly *exposed* to the weather. Simply put, Froelich was nude. Though he'd been fully attired when he'd ascended the ladder, that had been many years ago. Over the course of time, it had all come off. He'd grown tired of being presentable—and for whom, exactly? The birds? First he shed the socks and shoes, to gain a better grip on the rungs. His shirt he discarded on a bright, sunny day, and his pants after a poor night's sleep. Finally he climbed out of his undergarments—borne on the breeze like a petulant cloud.

Up the rungs, the elements could be unstable; consequently, the changing weather was his favorite topic. Froelich liked to ruminate on how the wind could play tricks with his ears. Without any landscape to influence it, a gust could travel for thousands of miles without interruption. Froelich had reported hearing uproarious laughter, or even weeping. He'd been audience to distant symphonies and stray bits of conversation. Of course, it all could've been in his head, the product of acoustics and loneliness. The man was subject to tempestuous rain, at any time and coming from any angle, often without warning. Hail storms, unobstructed sunlight—it was a regimen that no physician would prescribe.

As such, Froelich was constantly *under* the weather. It was for this reason that he kept a seasonal garden somewhere in the hundred-rungs, cultivating tiny fissures in the wood: pennyroyal, wintergreen, and yarrow, herbs for every ache and pain. Thinking, on that fateful day, that he had a fever, he'd decided to chew some ginger root. Unbeknownst to Froelich, the source of his torment had been an inner-ear infection. To further compound his error, he'd mistakenly climbed up instead of down.

In climbing argot, forward-and-backward was different from up-and-down. A person suffering from vertigo (as the result of an inner-ear infection) might have experienced dizziness, nausea, and spatial distortion—and while he might not have walked backward, say, instead of forward, Froelich, disoriented, had thought he was climbing down instead of up. After a little while, he'd even begun to wonder if he'd entered the two-hundred-rungs. If so, why didn't anything look familiar?

Having already come this far (and nowhere near the two-hundred-rungs), Froelich had failed to diagnose himself. Indeed, he'd forgotten all about his headache and his herb garden, and had decided he must be dreaming. After all, what did a person dream about, when he spent all his days on a ladder? He dreamed of climbing, of course.

Soon he'd reached the three-hundred-rungs, whereupon the clouds resided. It was common knowledge to the residents of Oregon that they received a disproportionate amount of rain; accordingly, their clouds were larger and fluffier than elsewhere. Denser, too—more thoroughly saturated. Certainly, they traveled in larger shoals, especially during the migratory season. It was rare for Froelich to climb so high as to see them, but there'd been talk, once, of collaborating on a lithograph, under the title "Whales of the Sky" (Froelich would've dictated while Binx transcribed). From the research Froelich had conducted, he knew that clouds molted. He knew that they migrated east and west between breeding and wintering grounds, and that they primarily ate pollen. Because they lacked teeth to aid in digestion, and because their stomachs were semi-permeable, they mostly abstained from eating meat; however, should a cloud chance upon a wounded animal, it had been known to take advantage.

In all likelihood, the cloud that poached Froelich had been a hungry and isolated calf. Why else would it have sunk so low, when clouds rarely ventured below two thousand meters, for fear of getting mired in the soupy atmosphere? To the cloud's eyes (sightless appendages, able to register only heat and density), Froelich must've resembled a molted bird, incapable of flight, or else a hatchling, having recently escaped from the nest. In either case, the cloud had entombed its prey.

Froelich, still feverish, had surrendered himself to it. Indeed, when a person spent all his days on a ladder, what did he covet above all else? The chance to lie down, of course. The thought of a bed had consumed him since his initial ascent, and not just any bed: specifically, the bed that Harald and Lotsee had shared. Froelich had obsessed over every detail—whether it was a mattress of straw or feathers, whether their blankets were burlap or wool. Of course, Harald had tried to assuage him via TAP, professing his great love for Lotsee while never once apologizing for his actions. But Froelich had refused to come down until the affair was called off. A year had passed, and Gordy had been born. Another year had passed, and Lotsee had died while birthing Binx. She might've thought that marrying Death would postpone the inevitable, and perhaps it had; but just as those under-rung had to enter into life, so too did they exit it, occasionally in the same messy turn of events.

It was in his compromised state that Froelich re-
visited those bygone days. When his fever did finally
break and he returned to his senses, the first thing he
became aware of was his position: supine, like a swim-
mer buoyed by water. Slowly, it dawned on him that
he wasn't holding on to anything. Paddling his arms
and legs, one hand emerged from the belly of the cloud,
where the air was shockingly cold. Turning his head, he
saw a blinding white light.

Am I dead? he wondered. *Frau Holda, have you mistak-
en me for an unbaptized babe? Granted, my a— is bare and
my feet are wrinkled, but didn't you notice the hair on my
face, not to mention elsewhere? When we were young, Harald
and I would share stories about you—how you rewarded the
meek handmaiden with gold, but slathered the lazy one in tar.
Harald was enthralled by the Wild Hunt, and how you'd ride
ahead to warn travelers, but I had my own questions about
Walpurgis Night. Were you there, too, Holda, among the other witches? If I reached out my hand to you right now, would
I touch your distaff? Not to abandon the old traditions, but
wouldn't a broom be more comfortable to ride upon?*

Froelich looked to the side and caught a glimpse
of the Earth. All at once, he felt alert—neither feverish,
dreaming, nor deceased. More so than your average
person, he possessed a unique appreciation of height.
From this distance, he knew he wouldn't survive a fall.
Where he presently found himself, there was hardly
enough oxygen to breathe.

D—ned stupid cloud! he raged. *D—ned stupid, hungry
cloud!*

If a seagull could pierce a cloud's surface with little effort, what damage could a grown man do? Indeed, it was for this reason that clouds were reluctant herbivores: not by choice, but of necessity. While Froelich punched, gnawed, and kicked at its interior, the calf produced a mewling sound, like an infant bleating for its mother.

Oh, you don't like that? I'll tell you what I don't like—being snatched from my ladder like a babe from its crib! Is that what you thought? That I was some tender morsel to be carried off and consumed? Well, let me inform you, cloud—this babe was weaned on splinters and nails!

Shredding another clump, Froelich accidentally removed too much. Suddenly, his support eroded. As the cloud's canopy sagged, his pelvis tilted and his shoulders slouched up around his ears—and for one queasy-making moment Froelich and gravity became newly acquainted, before his frantically grasping hands snagged a piece of hail and he was able to pull himself to safety. Even then, he didn't let go, hugging the rough sediment for all he was worth. His hands were shaking and his toes were numb. His bladder had unceremoniously purged itself.

Despite all his days on the rungs, Froelich had never worried about falling before. Whenever he'd considered the inevitability of his death, it had been in the most abstract terms. Now he was forced to recognize the immediacy of his situation.

Perhaps, he allowed, *I let my temper get the best of me. Forgive me, cloud, for being so rash—just as I will forgive you for trying to eat me. It's not easy to fend for oneself, is it? But now we have each other, for better or worse. Let's see if we can't resolve this situation amicably, and to everyone's satisfaction.*

Aside from his newfound (and circumstantial) compassion, something else had resulted from his tantrum: by the slightest of increments, Froelich's cloud had sunk in the sky. This was not inconsequential. From the port bow of his vessel, on its current, westward trajectory, Froelich could see the Pacific Ocean. Would that he were traveling east, he could attempt landfall, but his cloud was pointed west. With the forest giving way to pastures and marshland, he would soon be over water, at which point there'd be no recourse. What he needed to do was to reduce the cloud's altitude. This could be accomplished, he thought, if he sloughed off a little at a time; too much, and he'd risk compromising his safety. Poking his hand out the top, he released another tuft into the breeze.

Just a dollop, he assured the cloud, while also attempting to pet its flank. *Just a smidge. Not so much that you'll miss it, but enough to get home for dinner. My hero's tale doesn't end here, cloud—not smashed to pieces against the Oregon coast. So once more—just a dollop, just a smidge . . .*

CHAPTER 9

By the end of the first day, Binx was so hungry that he ate bugs. This was only after he'd polished off the remains of Miss Sarah's breakfast, and even after he'd gnawed on a pine cone. It wasn't that he was opposed to eating insects; Froelich, he knew, often augmented his diet with June bugs, dragonflies, or crickets—anything he could get his hands on. It was that, for a man of Binx's size, such modest portions only made his hunger worse. His stomach seized upon the promise of nutrients, and rightfully demanded more.

Beyond the caterwauls originating from his gut, his state of mind had made him overly sensitive. It was as if his body were a dreadful symphony, each singular discomfort acting in concert with the others: the crick in his neck sent pangs down his spine, to where his back felt constricted by an invisible corset. The swelling in his feet and knees pulsed in time with his headache—exacerbated, no doubt, by his appetite, but caused by the shafts of light cleaving through the trees.

Most disheartening was the mishap with the commode. In Gordy's absence, there'd been no one to empty the pot. Even stretching as far as he could, Binx couldn't distance it any farther away than a yard; thus, from his height, he'd had little choice but to stare down at its contents. Even if he were to shut his eyes (all the better to combat the light), *the* stench had been overpowering. For all these reasons, and to make himself feel less helpless, he'd attempted to nudge it with his foot and had succeeded in tipping it over. At once, the smell had worsened. The sight, if possible, had become even less palatable. With a bellow of frustration, he'd kicked dirt and nettles over the affected area—not that it had improved his situation.

When evening came and there was no one to light a fire, the forest sounded more savage than he'd ever known. Typically, Gordy slept in Lotsee's cottage, snoring loud enough to affect Binx's sleep. But now, trying to doze without it, Binx found that he missed the sound. In all these years, they'd never spent a night apart. As he continued to listen, rodents skittered through the underbrush, while owls conspired with one another. Off in the distance, a downed limb crashed through the tree canopy, followed by a second and a third, giving the impression of a drunken giant staggering home.

Hours before the dawn it unexpectedly rained. One moment, Binx was quasi-asleep, dreaming of goose-feather pillows; the next, he was soaked to the bone, his clothes clinging to his body and his feet bobbing in his shoes like pieces of cork. As suddenly as the storm had arrived, it had passed—every living thing, Binx included, equally stunned and affronted. His teeth began to chatter. Shortly thereafter, his entire body was ravaged by quakes, the muscles in his back clenching even tighter than before, while the stiles swayed perilously above him.

So it was, at first light of their second day apart, that Binx found himself tired, sore, and feverish. Though the rain had washed the earth, there was still a stain where the commode had tipped over. As a thick layer of fog carpeted the meadow, it suddenly occurred to Binx that Gordy might be dead. There was nothing to substantiate this idea, just a feeling of dread that came over him. If he'd been abandoned, he'd likely starve to death, or even die of chill. Without Gordy and Froelich, Binx was alone, save for this stupid ladder weighing against his back. Why was he even holding it up, if not for his uncle at the very top? He needn't starve, not with Miss Sarah's farm only a short distance away. He didn't trust his thoughts to be lucid after his phantasmagoric night, but didn't it beg the question? If Binx weren't supporting the ladder for Froelich, then for whom was he holding it? Himself?

While still exploring the contours of this thought, he heard a noise from behind him: twigs snapping underfoot and branches being shunted aside. Binx felt a thrill of relief. It was Gordy, safely returned! But after a moment's hope he soon realized his folly. Gordy, who always walked barefoot, wouldn't make such a racket. What's more, he'd never approach from Binx's rear, where he knew he couldn't be seen. Twisting and turning his head, despite the pain that it caused him, Binx tried to gain a better perspective, but could see no farther than the upturned commode.

Finally, a person emerged from the forest, standing in the meadow and grumbling to himself. From the coarseness of his voice, Binx could tell that it was a man. Wheezing and coughing, the fellow cleared his chest and spat on the ground.

"Hello!" Binx called out with false bravado. He knew it was pointless, but still he continued to crane his neck, first one way and then the other. "Good day, sir! My name is Binx. Please come around so we may speak face-to-face."

Though the smell of the commode was foremost in his nostrils, Binx now detected a different odor: practically feral, with a curious hint of cinnamon. Recalling the myriad noises from the night before, the thought entered his head that perhaps this was some kind of beast—a moose, possibly, or a bear. But, no, an animal wouldn't expectorate.

"Friend," he said again. "I'm afraid I can't see you. If you could come a little closer, we could be introduced."

Binx was wearing an insipid smile, from cheek to bearded cheek. He knew it couldn't be observed, but surely it made him sound more Christian. The smile faded, however, when he heard the person adjust his

clothing and then the unmistakable sound of urina-
tion. A torrent issued forth, hissing where it lashed at
the ground, and carried on for a ludicrously long time.
When at last it had been reduced to a trickle, the person sighed—giving his appendage a floppy shake before adjusting his clothing. He then resumed his march,
crossing the meadow and starting to climb the ladder.

"Hey!" Binx gasped, his hips protesting under the
weight of another person—a person who was not his
uncle or brother. "What're you doing? Get off!"

He witnessed a hand go past his eye, its nails chewed
to the quick. When a deerskin boot appeared to his left,
Binx slammed a fist down on it, eliciting a roar. Groping
between the rungs, he felt for anything he could grasp—
his fingers encountering an ankle and clamping down.
Though it was ungainly, the angle worked to his advantage. Binx could straighten his arm and exert a downward pressure on the climber. Thus, despite his best
efforts, the adversary couldn't ascend any higher. Binx
tugged and he pulled, until at last, with one final yank,
he was able to dislodge the stranger, who collapsed to
the ground in a terrific heap.

"Miscreant!" a wheedling voice decreed. "Imbecile!
How dare you treat Lord John like this?"

Binx was still trying to catch his breath. He doubted
he'd prevail again, should the stranger mount a second
offensive.

"What lord would climb someone else's ladder?" He
challenged the speaker, hoping to steer their contest toward a debate. "What lord that you know of?"

"Someone else's ladder?"

Laced with indignity, the voice became even more shrill. Picking himself up and dusting himself off, this Lord John circled the stiles to draw within poking distance. Much to Binx's surprise, they nearly stood eye-to-eye. Apart from his father, he'd never faced a man of comparable height. Furthermore, Lord John was endowed with an equally robust beard, though his was as white as birch bark. It was there that the similarities ended, Binx's opposite wearing a burlap tunic, a shapeless hat, and boots that laced as high as his knees.

"I say," Lord John stuck a finger in his face, "my land, my ladder. My right. My dominion. Only a fool or a knave would suggest otherwise. So which one is it, lad? Be ye a fool or a knave?"

Before Binx could speak, a word echoed from the back of his mind: Rübezahl. From Harald's folktales, he recognized the creature as king of the mountain (Rübezahl being a derisive term, from the German word for turnip), equally disposed toward charity or trickery, depending on the people he encountered. Of course, this was all a genial fiction, conceived of for children. But here he stood, his tunic barely long enough to conceal his manhood.

"Your land?" Binx said. "I was under the impression it belonged to my father."

"My dominion," Lord John repeated, throwing his arms open wide, to encompass the meadow and beyond. "No rational man would refute me. Were I to climb up that ladder of yours, I might see how far it reached. Will you let me pass? Or will you hinder me again?"

"My ladder—so you admit it belongs to me?"

For a contemplative moment, Lord John simply stared at him. Then, grumbling, he asked, "Where shall I sit?"

"What?"

"Sit, boy, sit! Where shall I sit? My legs are tired, and I don't fancy lying on the ground."

Binx indicated a tree stump on the opposite side of the campfire. It was where Gordy often reclined when he wanted to rest his feet. Thus positioned so low to the ground, Lord John resembled nothing so much as a porcupine—all elbows and knees, jutting out at sharp angles.

"Better," he said, running his hands through his beard. "Now, do you truly claim to own it?"

"Own what?"

"That ladder? Would you really claim it as your own?"

With a great show of looking around the meadow, Binx chuffed. "I don't see anyone else here. Do you?"

"Is that not Froelich up the rungs?" Lord John inquired, raising a finger toward the heavens. "Or don't you count him, for the purposes of our conversation?"

Binx was stunned. Opening and closing his mouth, he could think of no coherent reply.

"So you *do* count him," the Rübezahl confirmed, seemingly pleased by his agitation. "How generous. I'm sure Froelich would appreciate it."

"How do you know?"

"About Froelich? My dominion, my leasehold—every rock, every blade of grass. Nor have I forgotten about you, from our previous encounter. Be ye not Harald?"

This question affected Binx like a punch to the gut; had it not been for the ladder, he might've sat down, too. Meanwhile, Lord John continued to stare at him—thoughtfully stroking his beard, while combing out the occasional tangle.

"Not Harald," Binx finally replied, his voice barely louder than a whisper. "His son."

Squinting, Lord John leaned forward. "Yes, I see it now. Foolish of me to make that mistake."

"But you knew him? My father?"

"I met him once, years ago, when he first arrived—before he and your uncle discovered the Very Big Tree. Did you know, by your age Harald had already traveled halfway around the world? And what have you done? Where have you gone? If you traveled twenty feet, it would be an accomplishment! Froelich left his ancestral land, and what did Harald do? Like any good brother, he followed after him. Gordy climbs straight up into the air, and what do you do? Sit around all day, waiting. Like always."

Whether as a result of hunger or shame, Binx was starting to feel light-headed. He pressed his palms to his temples and said, "But—how do you know Gordy?"

"My land!" Lord John bellowed. "My dominion! I know every tenant. Every doe and fern, every thistle and berry. I know where the blue herons roost and the still water pools. You think I don't know Gordy? I was there to see him whelped. When he visits Miss Sarah,

I occasionally walk along beside him. Believe me, if I could converse with him right now instead of you, I'd do it in a heartbeat!"

"Did you know Lotsee?"

Smiling, Lord John rested his elbows upon his knees, his tunic shifting uncomfortably high. "A clever girl," he said. "Mad, too, but that can't be helped. When she signed her lease, she negotiated a shorter term. Five years—good for a woodland rodent, perhaps, but unheard of for a person. Did you know, it was your mother who taught me how to sew? If not for her, I'd be walking around naked! I was saddened to hear of her passing— but aren't you responsible for that, too? Good grief, man, is there anything you've not defiled?"

Despite the seemingly rhetorical nature of the question, Lord John awaited a reply. When Binx neglected to answer (truly, what could he say in his defense?), Lord John stood up and stretched. Then, lifting his nose to the breeze, he sniffed.

So fast that it defied comprehension, he'd crossed the meadow and thrust his hand amid the shrubbery. There was a general commotion while he rooted around, and when he extracted his fist it contained a bird—the head and feet poking out, squirming and bobbing like a windup toy.

"Sparrow," he said, then asking Binx, "Are you hungry?"

Binx was famished. But the thought of roasting the bird and how long it would take, plus what little, greasy meat it would produce, made him feel even more ravenous, not less so. Thus, with a dejected sigh, he shook his head.

"Suit yourself." Still holding the sparrow in one hand, the Rübezahl chomped its head off. The sound of bones crunching between teeth was more terrible than Binx could've imagined, the blood on his chin like the juice of some foul berry. Though Binx was sickened by the sight, his stomach also growled.

"You know TAP?" Lord John asked, through a mouthful of feathers.

"Of course," Binx muttered, lowering his eyes.

Gesticulating with the bird's corpse, the Rübezahl said, "Relay this message, then. 'My dear friend Froelich. Greetings! It's been too long since we last communicated. I trust you are well, and all is jolly up the ladder. As the anniversary of your leasehold approaches, let us renew our friendship and speak of matters great and small. Please descend to the lower rungs, where I'd be happy to see your face. If not, I can climb to you. However you are disposed, do me the favor of a timely reply. Yours in perpetuity, Lord John.'"

Only devoting a portion of his attention to the words, Binx continued to stare at the ground—specifically, at where his commode had been recently spilled. Much to his surprise, the soil there betrayed no discoloration. In fact, the commode was resting where it should be—empty and clean, like it had never known a day's use.

"I say, did you get all that?"

He looked up at Lord John. The bird was gone, the Rübezahl noisily licking his fingers.

"No," Binx stammered. "But it wouldn't make any difference. Froelich—"

"Ach! Never mind—you're as worthless as you are stupid! I'll relay the message myself."

Stomping his feet against the ground some meters away, he began to produce a series of vibrations, these vibrations forming words and phrases. The experience of having them pass through him, rather than originate at his own hand, was deeply discomfiting to Binx, like being turned into a ventriloquist's dummy.

"Stop it! He's not there—he can't hear you!"

"What do you mean, *not there*?"

"Since yesterday," Binx insisted. "Froelich's missing."

This revelation stopped Lord John in mid-stomp, his deerskin boot poised above the ground. As the Rübezahl lowered his foot, Binx looked for any sign of recognition, whether he might appear shocked, scared, or even content. But Lord John was impassive—listless, even.

"Did you hear me?" he said again. "Froelich is missing!"

Though the Rübezahl's expression remained placid, something was amiss; there was a strange energy in the air, a stirring among the low-limbed trees. A breeze buffeted Lord John's tunic, filling it like a mainsail. With a dry swallow, Binx swiped his palms against his thighs and realized that his hands were shaking.

Gently, as if to himself, Lord John commented, "Froelich is up the rungs."

"No," Binx insisted, "he's not." But he didn't have time to elaborate: a flash of lightning blanched the sky.

Somehow, inexplicably, Lord John was the source of this disturbance. Binx could feel a current coming off him, the dry air charged with electricity. Could Froelich feel it, too, he absently wondered, high above the ground and clinging to the stiles? But, no, Froelich wasn't there.

"Froelich is up the rungs!" Lord John roared. All at once, his face had become animated and he was in motion, rampaging toward Binx with his arms outstretched. "Without Froelich, there can be no ladder!" the Rübezahl bellowed. "Without the ladder, there can be no meaning! Froelich is up the rungs! *Froelich is up the rungs!*"

When he'd come close enough, Binx expected to feel those hands close around his throat. He readied himself to withstand such an assault, to the extent that he was able. But instead of causing him any harm, Lord John grabbed the stiles. Binx could see marrow stuck in the Rübezahl's teeth, and smell the rank odor of blood on his breath.

Thunder crashed. It seemed as if the whole universe would come toppling down. And, oh, how the ladder shook. The stiles warped at the very highest levels, a strange warbling effect that sent reverberations down Binx's spine. In Lord John's eyes, he could see madness, chaos. Binx recognized his own face reflected there, and understood an elemental truth: without Froelich there could be nothing—but without Binx there could be no Froelich.

Binx was at the center of it all, he suddenly realized, not Froelich.

The ladder trembled and the storm raged.

CHAPTER 10

Throughout the morning, Josie wandered down the beach without seeing another soul. On the bluffs high above, trees stood gnarled and slanted, a consequence of the easterly winds. In all likelihood, she was walking parallel to the Reservation, but how would she know? The sight of a solitary tepee, perhaps, or else a puff of smoke? The previous summer in Edinburgh, she'd been placed in charge of the Cowboys & Injuns sale at Jenner's Department Store. Frequenting the library for research, she'd crafted a chieftain and a squaw for the window display. The gent she'd adorned with a feather headdress, while his missus she'd provided a woolen blanket. Of course, Mae had made a mockery of Josie's work—sticking a feather in her own hair, and fluting a palm over her mouth. But how could Josie remain cross, especially to hear her laugh?

Ah, Mae Canby: what a ruckus they'd made, if only for the pleasure of each other's company. Josie had had friends before, but never like Mae. Always at each other's side, a voice in each other's ear, they'd shared clothes, shared a bed, even shared infections—first when Mae had contracted chicken pox, and later when Josie had caught the mumps. Their mothers had tolerated their kinship, distributing the burden equally—meals at each other's houses, holidays in Argyllshire.

As they'd grown to womanhood, their exploits had become more mature. The Saint Andrew's dance, for instance—hadn't that been their finest hour? Disinclined to bring a date, but determined to kiss the saltire at midnight, they'd each decided to escort the other. But how would that work, they'd wondered? One could imagine the looks on the Sisters' faces. The solution, Josie and Mae had decided, was Danny Foye: a single date for them to share, and not even a proper date at that.

"Say, Danny," Josie had said, sidling up next to him while he loafed home from school. "Why don'tcha ask me to the Saint Andrew's dance? I've already got my dress picked out. It's kelly green, with a modern bustle. Have you got a hat, Danny, or can you borrow one from your da?"

"No, Danny!" Mae had stomped her foot, materializing on the other side of him and passing her arm through his. "You told me we'd go! I've got my dress picked out, too—off the shoulder, to go with my gloves. Oh, but do ask your da for his ascot to wear."

"Oh, yes, do!" Josie had assented, barely keeping

herself from laughing. "And a stickpin to match."

Poor Danny Foye, with his weak chin and his sweaty palms. Content to do as he was told (his eyes as wide as saucers), he'd played the part and worn his father's ill-fitting suit. Together, all three had entered the parish house—everyone's eyes trained on this scandalous trio, no less so with Mae's shoulders exposed. When she'd handed Danny her stole, the other partygoers had gasped at the sight of her collarbone. Or perhaps it had been Josie's shortness of breath, and nobody else's.

The night had been mad, and would get madder still. Saint Andrew's cross had been fixed to the mantel, to prevent any witches from coming down the chimney. The Sisters in their habits stayed up well past their bedtimes, stifling yawns so wide they could've swallowed a dove. And whenever Mae danced close, she buried her hands in Josie's bustle, goosing and poking her until they were both cackling like jackdaws.

There'd been something else, too—a challenge issued under the laughter. Here, among these dancing, sweating, swarming bodies, and under the Sisters' drowsy gaze, who'd dare to risk the greater infraction? Whose lips might accidentally graze a cheek or an earlobe? Whose arms, raised in mirth, would come to rest around another one's neck? Had anyone acknowledged what transpired between them? Or had Josie herself imagined it? The smell of incense, and the sweat drying on her scalp, made it all seem like a dream.

Finally, when the clock struck midnight, but before they'd all braved the November cold, Josie had to rest her feet. Danny found her sitting in the nave, and offered her a drink of water. She hadn't seen him since they'd first arrived, or hadn't noticed him. He'd been disinclined to dance; rather, Danny had stood against the wall and tapped his toes. Maybe it passed for a good time. Or maybe not, and he tapped his toes nonetheless.

"Enjoying yourself?" he said, like he could read her mind.

"Indeed," Josie answered, still a bit winded. And then, because she would've willed it so, "And yourself?"

"Oh, aye. Me and the lads found a bag of marbles. I won a cat's eye at ringer."

"Sounds like a grand ol' time. Shame I didn't bring me jacks."

Instantly, his countenance turned stormy. "You think I'm daft," he said, "but I'm not."

"Oh, no—"

"It's all right—I don't care what you think. But tell me something else, since you're the one to ask? When's Mae's birthday?"

"Sorry, Danny, but it's come and gone. If you're looking to win her a steely, you'll just have to wait."

Again, he narrowed his eyes. Addressing Josie precisely, as if he were speaking to a halfwit, he said, "Her gloves are new—I doubt she's worn them before. She says they're a gift, so either her birthday's just passed or else she's been saving them. I'd like to know her kind, our Mae—does she virtue patience, or can't she wait? If you tell me her birthday, I'll sort it out for myself."

"February the fourteenth," Josie mumbled, feeling appropriately stricken. "Saint Valentine's Day."

Danny nodded, and began to walk away; but he couldn't, wouldn't, deny himself the opportunity to say, "D'you know what *your* kind is? The kind with a smart word—always something clever to say. Except, there's never a straight answer with you, is there, Josie? How is it you're so clever, when a person knows less for having talked to you? No, don't answer—I might swallow a marble on accident."

And to think, he'd called *her* clever. It was fair to say she'd misjudged him—Danny's wherewithal and the depth of his feelings. Josie would do well to take a lesson, and to find herself a feckless suitor at the Logging Camp. Rather that it was Danny walking down this beach, she mused—a penitent amid the looming sea stacks. In her head, he'd be forever confined to that stuffy nave. But he could have Mae pregnant by now, renting a flat over Charlotte Square, neither of them giving her a second thought.

Her tiff with Mae had occurred shortly after the dance. Prior to that, they'd been seeing less and less of each other, like she (Josie) had been contagious with something. *Tiff* was the word her da had used, and why not? Nothing in her own vocabulary had corresponded. Their row had been too significant for a misunderstanding, and too hurtful for a lark.

They'd been the last two at Jenner's Department Store one evening—dismantling the Nativity display, as chance would have it. "I've not seen you much," Josie said in an offhand manner, while ridding the manger of its motley tenants. "How've you been?"

"Oh, grand," Mae replied.

"Me, too—grand. So . . . you've been around?"

Shrugging, she gathered drifts of cotton snow, to be used again for the Easter display. "Here and there. With people."

"What people?"

"You know something?" Mae said, squinting at Josie. "It would be all right to find your own friends—other friends, besides myself. It would be healthy."

"Oh, I've got gobs of friends," Josie fibbed. In fact, they'd used to mock the girls who'd tallied acquaintances like charms on a bracelet; Josie had been proud to enumerate only one. Now, sorting the Magi, she tugged so hard on Balthazar that he sacrificed a limb.

"Oh, yeah? *Who*?"

"If you've got so many, maybe I can borrow one. Who've you been seeing, then?"

Mae cleared her throat. "Danny?"

"*Foye*? What'cha been doing with him?"

"I like Danny Foye! Anyway, he's nice to me."

"Of course he is—he thinks you're easy!"

Mae hefted a plaster cherub and hurled it in her direction, to be followed by one humpbacked camel and then another. For her part, even as she was avoiding projectiles, Josie immediately regretted the inference. Not so much an inference, even, as slander. If Danny enjoyed Mae's company, if he thought that she was pretty or kind, who better to empathize than Josie?

But once a thing had been said, it couldn't be unsaid.

"So what if he does?" Mae shouted, after exhausting her arsenal. "At least it's not unnatural!"

"Yeah? What's so natural about being groped?"

"You know what I mean," she hissed. "At least it's not a sin."

"Oh, so you're a nun now? Tell me, Mother Superior—when do you plan on being wed? Because if it's sin you're after—"

"What if we did? Huh? What if we did wed? Then I'd be *Mrs.* Danny Foye—and you'd still be an abomination!"

More words had been spoken after that, more accusations levied, but Josie couldn't recall the details. After being labeled a miscreant, she'd found herself trapped in the moment. Since then, she'd replayed their altercation many times, and it never improved, nor had they been able to remedy their friendship. Perhaps, had they remained on speaking terms, she might've reconsidered her decision that morning on the quay. Perhaps the lure of America wouldn't have seemed so great—the eccentric uncle and the chance to reinvent herself. Or perhaps not; it was unfair to speculate and impossible to know.

Either way, Josie hadn't been welcome at home anymore. If her row with Mae had been traumatizing, there weren't words for the schism between her and her mum. For some reason, Josie had never worried about her parents finding out. Maybe she'd been too heartsick to care, or else she'd been in denial. It had been a Tuesday afternoon; she could remember because she'd just got back from the chemist, renewing her da's prescription. When she'd walked though the door, angling for a hot cup of tea, she'd seen her mum standing inside the living room, her hands knotted tight. How long had she been there, staring at the door? Josie's first thought had been mistaken—that she'd been expecting her da, who must've done something wrong. But when her mum had barreled straight toward her, swinging her fists like mallets, her intent had been clear.

"Harlot!" she keened. "Strumpet!"

"Ow, Mum, you're hurting!" Josie shouted back, trying to protect her head. The coat and scarf she'd yet to remove provided some cushioning. "What're you on about? What's all this?"

"I just hosted Father Quinn, who got an earful from Moira Canby. I'm sure I'm the last to hear, save for your poor father—he's still down the pub. Would that he'd stay all night, and spare himself the trip back."

"*What*, Mum?"

By this time, Josie had escaped the narrow confines of the parlor and had placed the dining room table between them. Both women had been red-faced and breathless, standing before their respective table settings.

"Mae confided. She was scared to bits, Moira said—scared that Danny wouldn't have her. Can you imagine that? A little s—t like Danny Foye, saying no to someone? Moira would've said as much, I'm sure. But she's got blinders when it comes to our Mae." Impersonating Mrs. Canby's nasal inflection, Josie's mum whined, "Won't have *you*? Why not? What makes him so high and mighty, that you're not good enough?"

In retrospect, it should've been obvious. But Josie seized on previous misdemeanors, instead—novelties that she and Mae had stolen, and petty lies they'd told. The painful reality of their falling out was like an abscess on her memory.

They'd been stationary for long enough that her mum got a second wind. Slowly, like a jungle cat, she began to circle the table, and Josie matched her step for step, always keeping its full diameter between them. With each slow revolution, they passed the assigned seatbacks for their Sunday dinner: Mum, Da, Josie, Father Quinn; Mum, Da, Josie, Father Quinn.

"Corrupted," her mum sneered. *"Interfered with.* Can you imagine those words in the mouth of a priest? Moira told Father Quinn, and he told me. You preyed on Mae—not once, but habitually. He said the Devil makes you do it. He's seen it before—when he was assigned to the Carlisle parish, and Dumfries. Young girls who'd fall sway, and spread their defilement one at a time."

Her fury had reached its pinnacle, white blotches appearing on her otherwise tomato face. Meanwhile, her eyes were as black as coal. Without question, she would've caused Josie lasting harm, had she drifted within reach.

Lucky, then, that Josie continued to move, even while a general numbness pervaded her body. For Mae to have said those things to Mrs. Canby she must've been protecting her interests. She would've received the same tongue-lashing, if not the lick of the belt—and who could have guessed what Father Quinn would require, by way of penance? All this for Danny Foye. What a sad, strange consolation he made.

"A man of the cloth!" Josie's mum thundered. "Sitting in *my* house, at *my* table—saying these things about *my* daughter! I wish I'd died, Jo—that Jesus could've delivered me then. But no, I won't be spared so easily."

"Mum—" she said, but that was all.

"Go—get out. I don't care where, but I won't have you here. I'm liable to commit an even greater sin."

Finally she stopped moving. Staring down at the cherrywood table, the candles all herded together in its center, her mum made an effort to collect the stray wisps of her hair—her complexion slowly returning to normal, with the exception of her lips, still puckered and white as a polar bear's arse. At that image, Josie snickered. Sweet, blessed Mae. Even now, her voice in Josie's ear.

"Get out! Out!"

And so she'd gone from that place. Josie had already grown accustomed to wandering the streets of Edinburgh, though the circus procession still remained in her future. Now, when it occurred to her that she couldn't go home, she'd quashed the thought down—walking, always walking, with her hands buried deep in her pockets.

It had been past suppertime when she'd found herself at The Hog in the Pound. Just as her mum predicted, her da had still been there, though he'd been oblivious to any turmoil at home. Nor had any of the regulars been wise to her plight. Making way, they brought Josie a glass of bitters when she slumped at his table. Who could've guessed what would become of her, had she not lied? A convent, perhaps, or a one-way ticket to London. Rather, she inveighed herself on her da's sympathy—his poor, stricken daughter, betrayed by her best and only friend in the world, all for the love of a boy. She'd even invoked Danny's name without vomiting.

On the beach, Josie pressed the heel of her palm against her eye. Her da, of course, was still in Edinburgh. So was her mum, and Mae—even Danny Foye, she presumed, would be living the life that he'd previously known. Everyone of consequence had stayed behind, while she, Josie, had been exiled. But whose fault was that? She hadn't been banished, so much as she'd fled. Looking back on her decision, she experienced a frustration so great that it bordered on mania.

Like a rambunctious pet, the Pacific wind pawed at her, and whipped the sea foam into a froth. Holding her stockings away from her body, Josie watched as they wriggled. It made her think of her once-capricious spirit—like the night of the Saint Andrew's dance, the last time she'd felt happy. Somehow, that memory remained pristine, unsullied by all else to follow. When released from her grip, her stockings made a quick escape, frolicking down the beach more carefree than Josie had ever been. *C'mon, Jo!* they seemed to say. *Come and be merry!* Skipping and traipsing, only grazing the sand, they hastened away. Hastened toward the Logging Camp.

CHAPTER 11

Morning had become afternoon, and the day brutally hot.

How long had they tarried on that road to the coast? Minutes? Hours? No other traffic had chanced upon them. Eventually, the driver had started to collect flies, and the horse had grown skittish. Even then, Gordy and Gak had failed to rouse themselves, neither acknowledging their surroundings nor each other.

For his part, Gordy was thinking of the letter that Gak had produced—the envelope from Colorado. What news had it contained, he wondered? Had its sender made a successful life for himself in that virgin territory, or was he burdened by unpardonable crimes? The letter itself lay somewhere among the others—past the inconvenient body in the road, and the terrible mess they'd created.

They might've lingered indefinitely were it not for the sound of the church bell. Upon hearing the chimes, they both raised their heads and made inadvertent eye contact. The sound was distant, but distinct; on and on it went, like a summons to judgment. Without uttering a word, Gordy and Gak stood. Pointedly, they didn't look at the driver, nor did they borrow his horse and carriage. All they carried with them was Gak's bag of provisions: the rock candy, taffy, and jerky.

Thus, they shambled along, remaining at arm's length and hardly ever speaking. In short order they arrived at a town, laid out on opposite sides of a wide thoroughfare. The first thing Gordy observed (aside from the passing resemblance to Boxboro) was the preponderance of flat land. Clearly, they'd left the forest behind, as the continent now gently inclined toward the sea. Second, he noticed that it was eerily quiet. Even the insects were hushed.

"Where's all the people?" Gak asked, plunging her fist into the bag of preserved goods. Her voice sounded hoarse from lack of use.

When Gordy ignored her, preferring to walk in silence rather than maintain the illusion of comity, Gak answered her own question: "Is it Sunday? Maybe they're in church."

Even in 1871, after statehood, gold, and Indian sequestration, it wasn't uncommon to find deserted towns. Whole communities could collapse with little or no warning. But here, all the buildings were pristine, and the boardwalk had been swept of animal tracks. Also, there was the sound of the church bells to explain, still ringing in their ears. As they walked past an all-too-familiar Myers & Co. Store, the road hooked sharply to the right.

Rounding the bend, Gordy was startled by a loud crashing noise. Gak raised her eyebrows. "That didn't come from no church."

Then they heard it again—not quite as momentous as before, but still an awful din. Continuing along the loping curve of the road, they ultimately arrived at a cul-de-sac. There, to their left, was the town's church, big enough to receive an entire congregation. (Indeed, from inside they could discern the cadence of a sermon.) Though the air was oppressively hot, its doors remained closed. Standing adjacent to the church was another building, equally large, but without any signage to designate its purpose. Its doors stood open.

"I guess—"

This time, the crash was so loud that they both leaped with fright. It came from the second edifice and was accompanied by a manic shouting: a single voice, though the words were unintelligible.

No sooner had Gak and Gordy landed on their feet than a man came out the door and striding toward them—the owner of the voice, slight of build, with curly red hair and pale skin. He was wearing pants and suspenders to match Gordy's own, though the man's cuffs reached comfortably past his ankles, with a high polish to his shoes.

"You!" he cried. "Lad! May I solicit your assistance?"

Gordy touched his sternum. "Me?"

"Yes, you!" With a smile, the man turned to Gak and apologized, "It's heavy lifting I require—I'm sure you're twice as sharp. I say, is that taffy you're eating?"

"What?"

"Saltwater taffy—is it taffy in your bag?"

"Maybe?" she replied, clutching her sack. "So?"

"*So*, it must've been purchased at a Myers & Co. Store. No one else stocks it north of Sacramento."

Taking note of the man's accent, Gordy asked, "Is someone in trouble? Do they need help?"

"That depends on your meaning," the curly-haired gentleman replied. "How do you define trouble? Or help? And whosoever constitutes someone?" Failing to explain himself any further, he spun around and stalked back inside. Though they waited for another crashing sound, the tumult (and cursing) seemed to have stopped.

"We don't have to go in," Gak said, the aforementioned taffy now plugged in her cheek.

"Do you know who that was?" Gordy murmured. "It's Francis Myers."

"You're sure?"

Without further comment, he started toward the building. A not-small part of him wished he could proceed alone—that Gak would stay behind, or find her own way. Every time he looked at her, he could feel the weight of the bludgeon, as if it were still in his hands. But he hadn't walked five feet when he could hear her in tow: the dry-leaf sound of her sack, and her jaw furiously working.

Once inside, they were initially disoriented by the waxed floor, like stepping onto an icy pond. The hall itself was long and high-ceilinged, with a half dozen lanterns strung together at the end.

"If I may be so bold," Myers inquired of Gak, calling over his shoulder, "where did you make your purchase? Was it here, in town?"

"Purchase?" She frowned. Then, remembering her saltwater taffy, she answered him, "Huntsville."

"Huntsville—I see. And how would you rate your experience there?"

"My what?"

Pausing halfway across the long hall, he turned to face her. Frank Myers didn't look like the richest man in Oregon, Gordy thought, but what would that look like? Proprietor of all the Myers & Co. stores, as well as Myers & Co., what he didn't outright own had been constructed with his lumber. Here was someone who could speak to fame and wealth, and he only seemed interested in Gak's snack.

"Did you find everything you were looking for?" Myers continued. "Was the Huntsville counterman courteous and polite? How about the aisles—would you call them orderly and clean? Would you go back a second time? Or is it already your Myers & Co. Store of choice?"

"It's a store," Gak firmly stated. "It was fine."

Myers snorted. "Better than *fine*, I hope. I'd like to think that when a person enters a Myers & Co. Store he—or she—can expect a rewarding experience, and that that expectation will be honored, whether in Bend, Salem, or even Huntsville!"

"What is this place?" Gordy asked, trying to insert himself into their conversation.

"We tried playing by natural light," Myers commented, turning away again. "But the shadows made a muck of it. Also, we were constrained by daylight hours. I'd like to have lamps installed—incandescent, like I saw last year on a visit to France. Truly awe-inspiring. And you—do you have a name?"

"Gordy," he said.

Glancing down at Gordy's feet, Myers observed, "You're not wearing any shoes."

It was a rather odd comment to make, like acknowledging one's forward-facing head. At a loss for words, Gordy simply shrugged.

"No bother!" Myers declared. "I can loan you a pair."

The opposite side of the hall had the benefit of being better illuminated. (Gordy could see where windows had been boarded shut, both cut into the walls and high above them on the ceiling.) The air was more acrid here, closer to the ambient glow, but they were better able to scrutinize their surroundings. The floor had been divided into two lanes, each one roughly three feet by sixty. At the terminus of each lane, where the lantern light was brightest, were two ghostly wedges, each formed by ten pegs and overseen by an attendant.

"What is this place?" Gordy asked a second time.

Handing him a pair of shoes, Myers gestured at the lanes. "Have you never bowled before? It's a game—for sport! The object is to knock down as many pins as you can."

"But . . . why?"

"For sport!" he repeated, grinning like a shill. "I had the alley built last winter—before that, they used the space for cattle auctions. Lord knows, I've tried to get the townspeople interested, but there's no luring them away from church and industry. Those two I hire by the hour," he said, indicating two Chinamen, who stood motionless in the shadows. "But they won't play against me, either."

"You called us here . . . for a game?"

"What could be more natural? What say you, Gordy— join me in a contest?"

The novelty of this proposition caught him off guard. Inhaling the gas lamp's poisonous fumes, and with sweat trickling down his back, he was stunned by the frivolity of Myers's offer. Not more than an hour ago, Gordy had killed a man, all thanks to Gak. And now he was being invited to bowl? What sort of grotesquery was this? Homicide in the morning and sport in the afternoon?

"Sure," he said, succumbing to the strangeness of it all. With some effort, he squished his feet into Myers's proffered shoes. Gordy hadn't worn loafers since the occasion of Harald's funeral, and the feeling was akin to a horse being shod.

"Those look a mite small," the Scotsman commented, after Gordy had taken a mincing step. "Still, it's better than falling on your arse. We can share a ball. Hopefully, your fingers will fit."

"My fingers?"

"I had it custom made—I have fine digits, you see. Young lady, may I suggest that you sit over there?"

At that, Gordy and Gak both froze. Gordy's hands, already slick from heat, began to sweat even more profusely. Would he be required to murder Myers, too? And what about the Chinamen in Myers's employ—must he dispatch them, as witnesses to a crime? He couldn't spend the rest of his life protecting Gak—who, even now, was staring at him, her eyes wide, the weight of her secret a burden between them.

Seemingly oblivious to their discomfort, Myers directed Gak to a wooden bench, then selected a bowling ball from a nearby shelf. The orb was dark as shale and the size of a person's head. Observing Myers's tensed arm and the strain upon his face, all Gordy could think of was wielding his bludgeon.

"Allow me to demonstrate the proper technique. As you can see, there are three holes, here." Cradling the ball in the crook of his arm, Myers poked his thumb and middle fingers into the openings, balancing the ball with a look of intense concentration. "Employing an underhanded motion, the bowler rolls the ball toward the pins. I suggest that you aim for the head pin. Lad, are you listening?"

"What?" Gordy blinked. "Yes—of course."

Facing his lane, Myers exhaled. With two broad strides, he approached the leftmost wedge, swinging his ball in a pendulous arc and releasing it no higher than his ankle. It glided down the lane at a predatory speed and met the pins with resounding force. The sound was so loud that Gak inhaled her taffy.

"The two and seven pins remain standing," Myers observed while thumping her on the back. "With my next bowl, I shall attempt to convert a spare."

As the attendants rushed to retrieve the pins, Gordy inquired, "Is it always so loud?"

"A person gets used to it."

"Isn't it dangerous?"

Myers appeared confounded by this statement. "Oh," he said, acknowledging the attendants. "You mean for them? Yes, I suppose so. But I've made them partial owners, in the event that we open to the public. Maybe you've heard the term *sweat equity*?"

"No," Gak scowled. "Maybe *you've* heard the term no-good huckster?"

The younger of the two attendants fetched the ball—steering it with his feet, and rolling it back down the lane. When he caught Gordy's eye, he gave a polite smile, then sprinted back to the remaining pins, where he assumed his position.

"Now, on to unfinished business," Myers decreed.

Just as before, he took three long strides in the direction of the pins, released the ball, and admired its progress. This time, it whispered past the rightmost pin, which abruptly launched itself into the air and collided with its counterpart.

"A baby split!" he shouted. Then, composing himself, he confided in Gordy, "I'd be even better with some practice—it's so inelegant, having to rely on a spare.

However, I *did* score ten points, plus the value of my next roll. Each turn consists of two rolls, ten turns total. Do as I do, and see if you can't enjoy yourself!"

Copying Myers's grip (a wholly unnatural three-finger pinch), Gordy found the ball to be much lighter than he expected. Mindful of his longer gait, he took an additional step back from the release point, began his motion, and swung his arm—the ball coming loose in midair, resulting in thumb-popping pain.

"Careful!" Myers scolded him. "You'll hurt the finish!"

"Sorry—it got stuck."

"Maybe don't stick your finger so deep," Gak said. "It ain't plum pie—you ain't Jack Horner."

"You could do better?"

"I couldn't do worse!"

Stalking across the floor with the bowling ball still cradled in his arms, Gordy hissed at her, "You and me aren't chummy, Gak, so why not keep your advice to yourself?"

Scowling, he returned to the top of the lane and nodded to the attendant. This time, he used only his fingertips, guiding the ball in the direction of his target (rather than throwing it). The results were much improved: the ball went forward, though it failed to connect with any of the pins. Instead, it veered to the right and struck a protective cushion, producing a muffled *thump*.

"Can I go again?"

"Yes, of course. Take as much practice as you like."

"So, what?" Gak interrogated their host, finding her

voice again. "You invite people over to bowl, then quiz them on their favorite Myers & Co. Store? What're you doing here, anyway? Ain't it a bit humble for a millionaire?"

If he was offended by her glibness, Myers didn't show it. "Oh, we don't *live* here. We reside at Fort Brogue, courtesy of the Sergeant Major. I only come down here for sport."

"Fort Rogue, you mean—like the river?"

He pinched the bridge of his nose and sighed. "No, not like the river. Fort *Brogue*."

"You ever bowl with any famous people?" Gordy asked, trying his best to sound blasé. "How about Johnny Appleseed? You ever meet him?"

"Chapman?" Myers sneered. "Before my time. A total buffoon, from what I've heard. Walked around in rags, preaching the gospel."

Gordy frowned, hugging his ball. "*Johnny Appleseed*. Most famous man in America? You can read about him in books."

"Let me tell you something," Myers said, raising his reedy voice. "There's little difference between fame and infamy. You know who I am—yes, you do, don't pretend. But my name's been in the papers only once, on the day I was born. It'll appear a second time on the day I die, but not under different circumstances. Money means discretion—fame is the opposite of that. If you have to choose, take the money."

"So," Gak said, after a lengthy silence. "Not a fan of apples, then?"

"Hardly. The world's a better place without him."

"Johnny Appleseed's dead?" Gordy gasped.

"In the ground these six and twenty years." With a shooing gesture, Myers encouraged him to bowl again.

Feeling appropriately chastened, Gordy concentrated on his next turn. With improved accuracy and force, he was able to strike the pins and subject the attendants to greater risk. And yet he wasn't nearly as good as Myers. He hadn't knocked down a plurality in a single try, and his aim was dubious at best. It seemed important that he impress his host—that he acquit himself well, if not actually win.

"Remind me, again?" he said. By now, he was drenched in sweat, his narrow shoes squeezing the arches of his feet. "Two rolls per turn, ten turns total?"

"That's the gist of it," Myers agreed.

"All right, then, let's go. Age before beauty, I always say."

Myers wiped his hands and retired to the lane, where the attendants were finished organizing the pins. Patiently, he waited for them to withdraw, or perhaps he was more focused on his impending bowl. When he did finally move, all the joints and levers of his body operated in harmony. The ball traversed the lane without making a sound, the pins dispersing like geese off a lake.

"Huzzah!" he shouted, jumping up and down and thrusting his fist in the air. "A strike! Ten points, plus the value of my next two rolls! Your turn."

Gordy accepted the ball with grim determination, managing to knock down three pins on his first try. But before they'd even come to rest (the foremost pin still spinning in the lane), he was loping to where the attendants waited—waving them over and exchanging a few words. It only lasted a moment, after which he retrieved his ball and resumed his position.

"One moment, lad," Myers said. "They haven't reset the pins yet."

"I told them not to."

Before he could object, Gordy went again. This time his ball collided with the foremost pin, horizontal on the floor, driving it into the wedge. The seven remaining pins were swept aside—aided, in no small part, by his first turn.

In the resulting silence, Gak was the first to speak. "That's a spare, ain't it?"

"It certainly is *not!*" Myers blustered. "The pins weren't reset—the turn doesn't count!"

With the confidence of someone who's checked his math twice, Gordy reminded him, "That's not what you said. I asked, two rolls per turn, ten turns total? And you said, 'That's the gist of it.' That's what you said—you didn't say anything about resetting the pins."

"Ten points," Gak repeated. "Plus his next roll."

Myers appraised Gordy, his empty hands flapping at his sides. It seemed the Scotsman was debating something with himself. "Goodness," he finally murmured. "Aren't you a quick study? No matter—keep your spare. I'll just take greater pleasure in beating you." But his confidence was betrayed by his next roll: far wide, missing everything but the protective cushion.

After that, the contest unfolded quickly and silently.

The Chinamen left the pins for Gordy, as per his request, and he went on to record spare after spare. For his part, Myers insisted on resetting the pins—and while he performed admirably, he couldn't possibly keep pace. Finally, after scoring the seventh frame, he laid down his pencil and sighed.

"I believe that'll suffice."

"Suffice?" Gordy echoed. "What d'you mean? You're tired of getting beat?"

From his pants pocket, Myers produced a watch fob. "Do you know the secret to running a successful business?" he asked. "Mitigating the customer's expectations."

"Say again?"

"Reducing the likelihood of disappointment." As if provoked by his inspection of the time, the church bells next door began to peal. Immediately, everyone clapped his or her hands over his or her ears, while the attendants started to clean up the pins.

"So, you won't play it out?" Gordy hollered. He felt disappointed that he'd failed to impress Myers, but even worse was the prospect of being left with Gak.

"Not unless I feel like being humiliated," the Scotsman confided, "which isn't without its virtues. But I don't, so I won't. You should challenge my niece, Josie, if you want a fair contest."

"WHAT?"

"Sorry," Myers shouted, backing toward the entrance at the far end of the hall. "I really must go. The circuit judge is a pious man, but he never stays at church longer than is required. I thank you for the lesson, young man. And you, young lady—thank you for your honesty! The next time I pass through Huntsville, I promise to personally visit your location."

As they were both witness, he turned on his heel and marched out the door. Moments later, Frank's silent partners also exited the building, the Chinamen making use of a concealed hatch. Suddenly, Gordy and Gak were alone again—the gas lamps sputtering, the shadows lapping their feet, and the bowling alley feeling like a proximate Hell.

CHAPTER 12

Were his predicament not so perilous, Froelich might've recommended the view: majestic trees rising from the Cascades and wildflowers blooming in swaths of indigo. Even his earache had subsided, though he'd have welcomed the pain to be back on the ladder. A day and night had passed in the ether, and thus far his efforts to reduce the cloud's altitude (in order that he might plummet from a less injurious height) had been negligible; still, he continued to slough off a little at a time.

Ahead, the Pacific Ocean was growing noticeably larger. Borne along by the slipstream, his cloud was fast approaching the Oregon coast—too fast, he determined. Doing some quick calculations, he reasoned that, at his current rate, he'd be over water before he was low enough to jump. The force of impact would likely stop his heart, prior to being swallowed by the sea.

Meanwhile, up ahead and approaching at an alarming speed (or, rather, remaining perfectly still, while Froelich approached it), Fort Brogue remained invisible. All Froelich could see was a mass of clouds, and not the turret that they clung to.

When his cloud did finally merge with the herd, the impact was gentle; Froelich only knew he'd stopped when his insides lurched. It was a temporary reprieve, he knew. Soon, his cloud would disengage and continue its westward journey. At the same time, Froelich thought, here was a chance to improve his situation. What was the worst thing that could happen to him—he might be expelled and die a little sooner? Planting both of his hands on the cloud's downy surface, he cautiously supported his weight.

"Farewell, my hungry friend," he said, while crawling forth. "I'm glad not to have been your meal. In time, I hope you can flourish. But *should* you die, at least the weather will improve just a little."

Lumped together and jostled by the breeze, the herd produced a curious noise. Too atonal to be mistaken for music, it seemed less the product of the individual clouds than that of friction caused between them. The sound most closely resembled wind chimes. How had he never heard this before? Hadn't his research been thorough enough? If he did somehow survive this experience, Froelich vowed to share his discovery with the world, either by dictating his lithograph or alerting the proper authorities. A newspaper reporter might even be interested; Froelich would be a local celebrity. The act of planning for his future gave him hope.

Passing from one cloud to the next, he also observed a change in temperature. As he continued on his elbows and knees, careful not to compromise the gossamer surface, a window suddenly appeared in the mist. Froelich gaped at it. Without question, it was a window, replete with a frame and shutters. Had he possibly lost his mind? Even so, *especially* if so, shouldn't he scamper through it, just to see what was on the other side? Presumably, anything he'd encounter would also be a product of his imagination. Nothing could hurt him that he hadn't conceived of himself.

Extricating oneself from a cloud was more difficult than he might've expected. First, he attempted a serpentine motion, then he tried thrashing. After neither technique proved to be successful, he conceded to bring the cloud with him, still adhering in clumps to his torso and limbs. Climbing over the windowsill, Froelich found himself in a bedroom that contained a wardrobe, a bookshelf, and a bed, as well as a writing desk devised from an end table and an oval rug that covered much of the floor. Clenching his toes, so accustomed to gripping the rungs, he generated a hot clutch of friction. It *felt* real. If he were crazy, then his toes were crazy. Also, his hips and knees, evenly distributing his weight and supported by a horizontal surface. His hips and knees, now reporting dull pains, were also crazy. That his madness would span from his brain to his heels was nice, in a way. If Froelich was crazy, it was with his entire being.

Brushing tufts of cloud from his shoulders, he allowed them to float to the ceiling. He recognized this room from the fairy tales of his youth. After a husband and wife are caught stealing radishes from a witch's garden, they must surrender their firstborn child in order to appease her. Here the purloined girl would age to adolescence, imprisoned in a high tower, the only entrance or egress to be made by her hair. It was cause for some concern that this room, in which he currently stood, also had a door. Since no door was mentioned in the original story, Froelich had to assume it was a contrivance of the mind. Whatever lurked beyond the sturdy wood, he had no desire to find out.

The bookshelf featured a handful of tomes, many in Greek and Latin. Also on the shelves, as well as the desk, were mementos from the seashore: rocks, shells, and petrified wood. Girls' clothing, arranged in the wardrobe, had been hung in orderly fashion—save for a shawl, which was tossed upon the mattress.

Ah, the mattress: he'd been eyeing it since he climbed through the window. On its surface, he could discern the impression of a sleeping form. "What harm would it do," Froelich reasoned aloud, "if I were to pull back the sheets? If I were to lie down with my eyes closed, say—who would begrudge me this one small pleasure? Anyone?"

From the moment his head touched the pillow, he experienced a feeling of profound calm. The cloud had been nice, but this . . . this was sublime. Finally, he could ignore his aching body and narrow his thoughts to just the *idea* of himself. Outside, he could hear the cloud music playing, and wondered if he hadn't actually gone insane. But who even cared? Froelich could be dead and d—ned, and it wouldn't matter. For the first time in years, he felt at ease.

Which made it all the more upsetting when the pounding began.

CHAPTER 13

Binx thought the ladder was going to fall. Lord John was shaking it so hard that dust was rising off the ground and leaves were displaying their undersides. And what if it did fall? Froelich wasn't up the rungs anymore; the ladder served no demonstrable purpose. It was just a meaningless totem—and, for all that, it was extremely heavy against Binx's back. Why not let it topple, once and for all?

Just as Binx was ready to surrender, Lord John stopped—still holding onto the rungs, though his attention had been diverted elsewhere. Binx could hear it, too, now that the rumbling had diminished and the trees had stopped their quivering: the sound of someone whistling a tune. He recognized the song as one of Miss Sarah's favorites.

Lord John bit his lip. Releasing the stiles, he took a

step back from Binx, the ladder already ten times lighter.

"Does she know about Froelich?" the Rübezahl asked. How he knew that Miss Sarah was a woman was a mystery, but Binx wearily nodded his head.

"She brings him lemon cakes," he said. "Even though he never comes down. Gordy and I eat them ourselves."

"Then you mustn't tell her," Lord John instructed. "Do you hear me, lad? She mustn't know that he's missing."

Disinclined to argue or even to care, Binx ignored him. The prospect of yet another conversation weighed on him—having to feign interest in Miss Sarah's words, and duly reply to her inquiries.

Lord John took a step back, to better inspect the stiles. "I'll climb the ladder," he said, his face pinched with concern, "just high enough to conceal myself. You relay anything of significance via TAP. When she's gone, alert me and I'll come back down."

Miss Sarah was drawing near; Binx could see flashes of her white apron through the veil of leaves and wondered if she had any food.

"Do you hear me, boy?"

"Yes, I hear you!" Binx snapped. "Get on with it already, why don't you?"

Taken aback by his brusqueness, Lord John started to say something, then thought better of it. Instead, he walked around to the other side of the ladder and started to climb. Groaning under his weight, Binx inadvisably glanced up, catching a glimpse of the Rübezahl's undercarriage.

"Don't forget about me," Lord John said as he ascended to the double-rungs. "Say you won't!"

"I won't forget," Binx muttered. Would that it could be so easy.

Moments later, Miss Sarah appeared with a picnic basket, its contents covered by a linen napkin. She wore an apron, a bonnet, and a denim skirt—the outfit he was most accustomed to seeing on her occasional visit, and which she'd worn even during their schoolhouse days. A year older than Binx, she'd tutored him when he fell behind in his subjects.

"Good morning, Binxy." From the look on her face, he could guess at his sorry state.

"Good morning, Miss Sarah. How are you?"

"Another day older," she said. With a cursory glance at the meadow, she inquired, "Where's Gordy?"

"He's off somewhere," Binx fibbed. "Fetching water. He'll be right back."

His lie was obvious; seen from another person's perspective, there could be no denying Binx's abandonment. The fire had been extinguished, the remnants of yesterday's breakfast lay scattered in the grass—and also, to Binx's surprise and dismay, the upturned commode remained spilled on the dirt, now smeared with rain.

Miss Sarah took another look-see, then said, "Really—just us? Then let me tidy up while he's gone. There's no reason for you to be uncomfortable."

"Please, don't," Binx insisted. "I—"

"You hush." Collecting dirty utensils from days past, she stashed her picnic basket at a prudent distance.

"Not another word on the subject. Tell me, have you had your breakfast yet?"

"No."

"Then I'll get the fire started. If Gordy comes back, he can join us."

Rather than face her, Binx continued to stare at the commode. With absolute, unequivocal certainty, he knew he'd seen it restored. He could also recall having kicked it over, but the former image was the more vibrant of the two: the simple elegance of its bone-white porcelain, the gentle curve of its turned lip. All that remained now was a day-old mess, with a cloud of flies for Miss Sarah to contend with.

How bad did Binx look, for what little attention she was paying him? He could feel her eyes shying away whenever she turned toward the stiles. The past twenty-four hours had been unkind to him, that much Binx already knew, but was his appearance much improved on a normal day? Quite suddenly, and fervently, he wished that Miss Sarah had stayed home this morning.

"Perhaps it's best that Gordy's away," she casually observed, as she gathered wood from the nearby log pile. "I can't remember the last time we spoke alone. Hiram wanted to come, too, but I told him to make an appointment. He has so many questions. He wants to interview Gordy about the ladder."

"Your cousin," Binx mumbled, recalling Gordy's enthusiasm from the day before. "The newspaper reporter."

"*Former* reporter," Miss Sarah stressed. "In Philadelphia. I'm not sure who he'll work for here. Maybe the *Oregon Spectator*?"

"Is that why you're here? To ask for an interview?"

Smiling, she said, "No—Hiram can manage his own affairs. What he *can't* do is make himself useful around the farm. I was hoping to ask Gordy to slaughter a pig for me."

Binx didn't respond to her supposition. Having lied about Gordy's whereabouts, he felt pained anew by the possibility of his death. Gordy was gone, Froelich was gone—even Lord John, Binx suspected, had been the product of his diseased mind. Meanwhile, Miss Sarah was having trouble lighting the firewood. It was still damp from the previous night's deluge, and refused to ignite. Finally, after producing much smoke and little warmth, she managed to nurture a flame, wiping her hands against her apron and grunting contentedly.

"I told him I didn't know very much," she continued, curating their conversation as if Binx were an active participant. "Hiram, I mean. He asked when the ladder was built and I said I didn't know—before I was born, I said. He asked how it was balanced and I mentioned you. But when he asked about your father and your uncle, I had to plead ignorance."

Though Binx had been listening for a question, he'd yet to hear one. Still, Miss Sarah continued to watch him expectantly, so he mentioned, "Harald held the ladder."

"Your father? I remember him a little. He was big, like you?"

Nodding unhappily, Binx blinked his eyes when the campfire smoke blew in his direction.

"What about your uncle, then? He must be smaller, for you to hold him on your back. My mother used to tell stories about Froelich—how he'd play practical jokes, like jumping out of trees at people. Is that true? Was he funny?"

At this point, Binx had reached the limits of his humility. He was aware of how bad he must smell. He didn't want to spend any more time discussing Froelich's antics, or Harald's stature, nor did he enjoy her persistence on the subject. But just as he was summoning up the words to say so, Miss Sarah began to dig a trough for the contents of his commode. Using a spade from the woodpile, and working on her hands and knees, she produced a shallow hole—nothing too fussy, just deep enough to dispose of the mess. Without so much as a sour face, she scraped the ground clean and covered it over.

"There," she said, tossing the spade aside and touching her forehead with the back of her hand. "You were saying?"

"Um," he mumbled, having lost some of his vitriol. "Funny? Yes, I suppose so. He, uh—sometimes he wouldn't tell me it's about to rain, just to see me get wet."

Miss Sarah frowned. "That doesn't sound funny."

"No, maybe not, but it's Froelich's idea of a joke. Or sometimes he'll drop things."

"From up there?" she said, shielding her eyes against the sun. "Wouldn't that be dangerous?"

Binx didn't have an answer for this, so instead he shrugged. It wasn't that he was doing a poor job of representing his uncle; rather, Froelich's behavior was oftentimes lacking. If Hiram wanted to paint a sympathetic portrait of him, he'd just have to be creative.

For her part, having seen to the fire and tidied the meadow, Miss Sarah now unwrapped her picnic basket. She poured a Mason jar of sausage gravy into the skillet—unwrapping a bundle of fresh biscuits, three or four of which she piled onto a plate. Binx's stomach whinnied like a spooked horse.

"We needn't wait for Gordy," she said. "Sausage gravy's your favorite, isn't it?"

Binx nodded, licking his lips. When Miss Sarah handed him a plate, he immediately devoured it, momentarily blinded to any social niceties. Taking a tiny bite of biscuit for herself, she moved the skillet to the edge of the flames.

"So, you inherited the ladder from your father. When was that?"

"Dunno." Slowing down a bit and muffling a burp, Binx surmised, "The spring before last?"

"What happened? He became too old?"

"Froelich dropped a chisel on his head."

As soon as the words had left his mouth, he realized what he'd done. Sneaking a glance at Miss Sarah, he confirmed her stunned silence—so Binx finished chewing his food to avoid further explanation. When she still didn't utter a word, just ogled him expectantly, he sighed and lowered his plate.

"You know what a chisel is?" he asked. "Froelich had one he considered lucky—though what made it lucky I really couldn't say. One day, just a normal day like to-day, it slipped from his hands. Gordy and I were set-ting snares, but the sound we heard—it was awful, like a rock striking a melon. We came running, but by the time we got here it was already too late. Harald's eye had turned red and the side of his face was all swollen."

"That's terrible!" Miss Sarah exclaimed—which, upon reflection, was probably true.

Things had proceeded swiftly from there. Even while the strength had ebbed from Harald's body, Binx had faced away from his father, positioning himself rear to rear, as if the stiles had been a pane of glass and the two of them were mirror images. They'd never discussed the possibility of Harald's death before, nor how such a transfer would take place, but Binx had moved without hesitation. Given a gentle nudge of his posterior, Harald had angled the ladder away from himself . . . and to-ward Binx. Thus tilted, the change had been made. It had never been conceived of as a permanent solution; Gordy hadn't been big enough, and Harald had been close to death. From Froelich's perspective, the change had been a matter of degrees. To Binx, the difference had been more substantial.

"Harald died the next day. He lasted through the night, but he never spoke another word—not to us and not to Froelich. We never told him, either," Binx said, scuffing his foot in the dirt.

"Who—Froelich? But didn't he hear the sound?"

With a feeble snicker, Binx admitted, "We said it was a chicken. *I* said—I told him the chisel hit a chicken, thanks very much. He wasn't sympathetic."

"So he doesn't know?"

Again, Binx scuffed his foot. The gravy was congealing on his plate, but he found that he'd lost his appetite.

"Then, if you never told him," Miss Sarah pressed, "does he still think your father's alive?"

"Of course he does—he thinks *I'm* Harald! He thinks we moved the ladder because, I don't know, it was blocking the sun. I can't even remember our excuse. He complained about it for days—on and on, about how we should've warned him, and how we owed him a new chisel. We kept thinking up different ways to say it—but eventually enough time had passed that we decided not to. Anyway, what did Froelich care? Lotsee was dead and he *still* hadn't forgiven Harald. For God's sake, he'd spent nearly half his life up the rungs!"

Binx stopped to catch his breath. The missing detail, of course, was Froelich's absence, as well as Gordy's effort to find him and *his* subsequent disappearance. He'd already said more than he'd intended, but finally the truth was out. Poor Harald, dead and gone these past two years, killed by the very brother he'd wronged. Poor Froelich, alienated from humanity, victim to whatever fate had befallen him. Poor Gordy, whereabouts unknown. And poor Binx; most of all, poor Binx.

The fire was burning low again. Retrieving another log from the pile, Miss Sarah tossed it on the pyre, filling the air with sparks.

"Monster."

She spoke the word with such sadness, it almost sounded like an apology. The accusation hit Binx hard. Not that he disagreed, necessarily, but Miss Sarah had always been sweet on him.

"You don't understand," he pleaded. "I didn't know what else to do! Maybe if there'd been someone to ask—"

"Not you," she interrupted. *"Him!"*

Blinking his eyes, he was slow to comprehend. "You mean Froelich? You think *he's* a monster?"

"Of course I do!" she fumed, snatching the tin plate from his hands and noisily adding it to the existing pile. "Anyone who'd murder his own brother—"

"To be fair," Binx clarified, "he didn't *mean* to murder him."

"No? What's he expect to happen when something falls—that it'll bounce? I'm sorry, Binxy—I know he's your uncle, but what he's done, how he's acted, it's utterly vile. He just—I don't—have I ever told you the story of my mother, from before we were born?"

When he shook his head, Miss Sarah continued, "Froelich and your father had some kind of argument, shortly after they'd arrived. Froelich was walking through the woods when he met my mother, picking mushrooms. She was already wed, but my father had gone South for the night. Well, Froelich took a shine to her. He said they should run away together, that he'd fallen madly in love."

Playing with the strap of her bonnet, which appeared to be chafing her throat, she ultimately pulled the whole thing off. Miss Sarah's hair was fine as corn silk—much like her own mother, Binx imagined, when she was young.

"She said no, of course," Miss Sarah chuckled. "But do you know what Froelich offered her? By way of an engagement gift? Firewood. He said he'd found an immense tree—the biggest tree she'd ever see. He said they never needed to be cold again, or scared of the dark. Can you imagine anything more ridiculous? She was a married, Christian woman!"

This last morsel was too big for Binx to swallow. Had Froelich been out gallivanting, even while Harald was carving the Very Big Tree? Tossing his plate on the ground, he said, "So, what? What shall I do—ask Froelich to beg forgiveness?"

"It's not my place to say."

"But what would *you* have me do?"

"Nothing, Binxy," she murmured. "I don't expect anything from you. I'm just here to ask Gordy for help."

With that comment, an awkward silence developed between them. Miss Sarah proceeded to stare at the trees, as if willing Gordy to magically appear, while Binx contemplated his discarded plate. And somewhere far above them, the Rübezahl clung to the ladder, even now surveying the extent of his domain.

CHAPTER 14

Having never visited the Logging Camp before, Josie was uncertain where it began. At some unspecified point, she'd traveled inland from the coast and had gotten herself lost among the trees. The air had become drier, like raw silk between her fingers; when she'd sneezed, there'd been blood on her hands. The moss absorbed any hint of sound, while far overhead an eagle pinwheeled in the periwinkle sky.

She'd assumed there'd be some invisible line to cross, whereupon the laws of Oregon (made and enforced by men like Uncle Francis) would be ceded to mob rule. How large a mob that might actually entail, and what sorts of laws they might choose to enforce, were the stuff of dark fantasy. But perhaps the line wasn't invisible, she found herself thinking, so much as it was self-enforced. One moment she felt certain she'd arrived—seeing a man, listless, beneath a tree. But the next minute she'd encounter a signpost, pointing the way toward California. Despite the occasional caravan she passed, shuttered against a polite knock, there was nobody to ask and nothing to consult. Just the quiet company of ancient things.

Perhaps her official arrival at the Logging Camp co-incided with the hole in her shoe. She'd stepped in a rel-atively benign puddle, and water had seeped between her toes. Josie cursed herself thrice as she removed the offending boot—first, for walking through the puddle, which she easily could've avoided; second, for remov-ing her stockings on the beach; and third for the pebble she now held in her hand. Pink, rounded, and smooth, she'd been walking on it these many miles to distract from her hunger. Holding the boot upside down, the hole appeared as big as halfpenny.

With little choice, she pulled it back on and continued her trek. In her urgency to find a cobbler, she became even more curious about the caravans now clumped in twos and threes, with chocks under their wheels and raised canopies. But nobody had a shingle out with a clear in-dicator of the services provided. One had to be a familiar, Josie realized, to know the proprietors—how long they'd occupied their stalls and what prices they charged. It was an economy for the well-informed, not tourists.

So far, there'd been no linear dimension to the set-tlement, no streets or avenues laid out in a grid. Some paths appeared better traveled than others, the plant life trod down from regular traffic, but even those trails could be harsh on her feet. The air smelled of damp ashes, and the occasional outpouring of laughter made Josie turn about. Clotheslines had been strung between the trees, swaying in the breeze and bearing the weight of sodden laundry. Where the lines were presently empty, they'd been marked with bright ribbons to prevent an unwitting pedestrian from garroting himself.

Finally, Josie picked a caravan to make her inquiry. She selected it above the others because it had recently been painted (green and red, like a yuletide gift), and because its steps were not so steep. As she approached the vehicle, there was movement from behind the curtains. Accordingly, a man emerged. He was sinewy and short, and moved with purpose, closing the door behind him and trotting down the stairs. While he wasn't wearing a suit, he remained presentable. His hair and moustache, Josie saw, had been styled with pomade.

"Good afternoon, miss," he said, speaking in a resonant voice. "How may I help you?"

"You don't happen to be a cobbler?" Josie asked. Leaning one hand against the lacquered caravan wall, she offered a view of the offending sole.

"As a matter of fact I am."

"You're not!" she guffawed, astounded by her luck. "Are you really?"

Frowning, he walked around to cradle her foot— Josie suddenly made aware of her bare knee.

"This is a good boot," he said.

"Yes, well—excluding the hole."

When he didn't immediately release her, she began

to feel uncomfortable, hopping on one leg while compelled to lean more heavily against the caravan. If she'd asked for a doctor, would he have claimed to be that, too? Or a cook, if she'd mentioned her hunger? Thankfully, the cobbler was receptive when she cleared her throat. He gently lowered her foot to the ground and retreated to an appropriate distance.

"I'd buy those from you," he stated, matter-of-factly. "Would you barter? But wait—you'll need another pair. Do you?"

"Do I what?" Josie frowned.

"Have another pair?"

Shaking her head, she said, "Only what you see. Are they really so fine?"

"It doesn't matter." Motioning for her to raise her foot again, the cobbler took another look at the hole. "I don't have anything in stock that might fit you. And I can't let you go without shoes, not in good conscience. You'll step on a nail."

Josie was mildly disappointed; furthermore, she was made to confront her lack of resources. How was she going to pay for food, or decent lodging? She hadn't considered such concerns when leaving Fort Brogue, and now found herself mildly alarmed. Since the day she'd arrived in America, her uncle had provided every material thing: food, shelter, and clothes. She didn't even have goods to barter with, as the cobbler had suggested—a shame, given all the trinkets in her turret.

At least she'd chanced upon an honest man. From her business dealings with Uncle Francis (endless visits to the Myers & Co. stores, each location a reflection of the last), Josie considered herself to be an excellent judge of character. The cobbler, for his lack of showmanship, struck her as a plain-dealer. As such, she resolved herself to be forthright:

"I don't have any money."

The cobbler shrugged. "They say it's the root of all evil. Besides, there's not much cash changing hands. I'll take an I.O.U."

The notion of an I.O.U. caused Josie to bristle. It was just another denomination in the imaginary economy, no better than a Confederate dollar. But since she had no other way to make a payment, there appeared to be little choice in the matter. Having never provided an I.O.U. before, she didn't know how to proceed—whether she should spit on her palm, or else provide a written receipt. Finally, she blurted out, "I owe you."

Apparently, an oral contract would suffice. With a nod, the cobbler started back up the stairs, saying, "Let's conduct our business outside. You don't want to enter my wagon unescorted—people will talk."

Watching him disappear inside his caravan, Josie snorted—but perhaps she should be more conscientious. After all, her reputation was the only currency she had left.

It required numerous trips for the cobbler to amass his various tools outside. Some items Josie could identify by sight: a compact cauldron for melting rubber, great iron tongs for handling a boot. But other things, and their nominal purpose, she couldn't have begun to guess—such as an array of glass ampoules, and something shaped like a wishbone. It was an impressive collection, to say the least. At a certain point, she wondered if he was taking *everything* out of his caravan in order to reorganize it. But after concluding his fourth circuit, he stopped to admire the mess.

"I hope there's nothing missing," she joked. Despite her attempt at humor, the cobbler's expression remained blank.

"No, I think we have everything we'll need. I'm just wondering if it's going to rain. I wouldn't want it to get wet—there's some very expensive equipment here."

Josie tried to imagine what might be most (or least) expensive. The sundry jars of shoe polish? Or the metal cast of a foot, flat like a duck's bill? Still, he underwent the tedious process of returning more than half the items inside the caravan. Meanwhile, Josie, her feet still aching from the long walk, decided to sit down. Smoothing her dress against her thighs, she reclined on a log with her knees pressed together, continuing to regret the absence of her stockings.

"What brings you here?" the cobbler asked, as he continued to separate the objects. He didn't seem particularly interested in her reply, not bothering to look up while he negotiated the clutter.

"A husband," she answered. Having said the word aloud, she felt a flutter of anxiety. Josie's idea of a champion had evolved over time, while walking down the stretch of beach. After all, why would a stranger come to her aid, or provide her with safe passage to Scotland?

Wouldn't it be easier to ask a spouse? Of course, it would require a groom of little or no guile, someone she could bend to her will. It would further require that Uncle Francis honor the contract, were he to discover them.

Briefly, the cobbler paused in his efforts. "You're here to be wed?" When she nodded, hoping to convey confidence, he grunted. "You'll need a license for that."

"A license?"

"A wedding license," he said. "I can make you one. Do you know your husband's name?"

That he'd think to ask such a thing demonstrated the cobbler's savvy. For her part, Josie should've been outraged—except, of course, she *didn't* know his name, nor whom she might marry. Having to choose between feigned outrage or the slightest tinge of embarrassment, she found that neither came to her naturally.

"Not yet," she said, making tiny circles in the air with her one good boot. "Is that a problem?"

The cobbler shrugged. "I can't see why. You can make one up. Or leave it blank, to fill it in later. That might be easier, depending."

"Depending on what?"

"On what's more important." He grinned. "The husband or the license?"

"Like the chicken or the egg," Josie laughed. She could appreciate the cobbler's discretion. At the same time, she didn't want to reveal herself too soon. "That's the riddle, isn't it?"

"It is, indeed."

Now that he'd stowed all the nonessential or

expensive equipment (and with no rain to show for it), the cobbler seemed exhausted. Rather than commencing his work, he too took a seat, dragging over an anvil and squatting comically low to the ground. Judging from his hands and eyes, Josie tried to make an accurate guess of his age: older than she, but not so old as Uncle Francis.

"Can I make an observation?" he said.

"I'd be delighted if you did."

"That hole in your boot is well-earned, but the heel's not as worn as the toe. However far you've traveled must've come all at once. Was it a long walk here?"

"It was," she replied, feeling as if she were playing a parlor game.

"Where are you coming from?"

Here Josie paused. The cobbler *seemed* like a decent fellow, but still he remained a stranger to her.

"May I ask you something first?" she replied. "What's your name?"

Sitting back, he thrust out his hand in introduction. "Danny."

Immediately, her mind summoned the image of Danny Foye. "No—it can't be! Really?"

"Have I said something funny?"

"Danny what?"

With his hand still extended, the cobbler—Danny—blinked. "Just Danny," he said. "There's no last names here."

"No last names. But there are wedding licenses and I.O.U.s? How can the latter be true without the former? What sort of magical place is this?"

Withdrawing his hand, he gave her a tight-lipped smile. "Let me see—nice clothes, looking for a husband. I'd guess you're pregnant, except for the boot. That's a long way to walk for someone who's expecting. Something else, then. Something bad."

Though she could feel herself shrinking, Josie fought to maintain eye contact. Was it really so obvious, she wondered? Or had she seen so little of the world that she couldn't guess the cobbler's story at a glance?

"*That's* why, Miss. No last names—it's survival, not magic."

"Josie," she finally said, offering her own hand.

"Josie," he repeated. Danny's palm, when clasped, was firm and dry. "A pleasure to meet you."

"Tell me—how long before you can fix my boot?"

Swiping that same strong hand across his face, he produced a weary sigh. "May I be honest with you? The truth is, I'm not *really* a cobbler—not by trade, anyway."

"But all those tools—"

"Either bartered for or won. Some have no use. Like that thing," he said, poking his toe at a hinged piece of metal. "I'm not entirely sure what it's for."

In light of this revelation, Josie expected herself to feel angry, or betrayed, but instead she found it to be inconsequential. Her boot still existed, as did the hole; nothing had fundamentally changed.

"So your offer to fix my shoe?"

"I stand by what I said—no pun intended! You can't walk around here barefoot, not if you plan to remain in good health. There's a real cobbler by the Chinese laundry—Morris, his name is. I can introduce you. He's oftentimes drunk, and he quarrels with his inventory, but he does good work."

With a nod of her head, Josie assented. "Let's go see him. And if it turns out *he's* not a real cobbler, then maybe he can point us toward someone else. And so on and so forth, until I've met everyone in this camp."

Rising from his anvil, Danny collected his stray pieces of artifice—most of which, Josie now observed, were obviously junk. In her willingness to believe him, she'd imbued everything with a false sense of purpose.

"Not to be rude," she said. "But what *is* your true profession?"

He coiled a length of rope in his hands and gave her a thoughtful look. "Contracts—I bring people together."

"Like you're doing now, with me and Morris? Is that your play?"

Grinning, he said, "When I've made my play, you'll know it." And, with that, he carried an armful of equipment back inside his caravan.

A snatch of song carried through the trees: two voices, slurred with drink, yowling about goober peas. Josie assumed the revelers must hail from a neighboring caravan, though it seemed unwise for her to leap to conclusions. How willing she'd been to believe Danny! In truth, she rather liked him—the unfortunate coincidence of his name notwithstanding. He reminded her of Uncle Francis. Bringing people together—wasn't that essentially what Uncle Francis did, except on a larger scale? Certainly, he had no qualms about stretching the truth.

Should circumstances permit, perhaps Josie might introduce the two. They could open a Myers & Co. Store at the Logging Camp and install Danny as manager. It was the kind of idea that made her worthy of promotion, if not adoption. Too bad Uncle Francis wasn't getting a son.

When the song reached her ears again, it sounded much closer than before. Rising from her log, Josie smoothed the fabric of her dress. Danny continued to tarry in his caravan, creating a great deal of noise, so she helped herself to a piece of equipment: the metal wishbone-looking thing, numbingly cold to the touch. When he came back outside, she could return it to him. In the meantime, Josie took some comfort in its heft.

Leaves rustled and parted, as strangers emerged from the foliage. The taller of the two, skinny to the point of being hunched, was looking intently at the caravan. The other man, whose rotund belly brought to mind a friar, was still humming a Rebel tune. Both men carried heavy cudgels.

"Well, look here, Nantz," said the friar, with an unfriendly smile. "Danny's got himself a friend. Hello, friend."

Before she could reply, the second man growled, "You said it, Carmichael. How about putting that down, friend, before your arm tires?"

Josie's eyes flitted toward the caravan, where she hoped to see Danny reappear. The two men stood on either side of her. She tried to imagine using the wishbone as a weapon, swinging it at the men's heads; when she found that she couldn't, she discarded it. The wind shuffled the leaves from green to white as the quality of light became opaque.

"Is he alone?" Carmichael asked, taking another step toward Josie. Nodding, she signaled in the affirmative, not trusting her voice.

"Good. Lemme tell you how it works. Me and Nantz is debt collectors—"

"*Expert* debt collectors," Nantz interrupted, his eyes on the caravan.

"Right you are—expert debt collectors—and Danny's debt is due. So we're gonna straighten him out while you wait here. You be sure to keep your pretty mouth shut." Leaning forward, he snarled, "Understood?"

Josie acquiesced, hugging her arms around her chest. Together, the two men approached the caravan, carelessly treading on strewn equipment. Danny was still engaged in whatever activity was delaying him; apparently, the noise he created had prevented him from overhearing their conversation. When the two men reached the steps, they swiftly breached the door, first Nantz and then Carmichael. There was a moment of silence, after which the caravan began to shake, all three voices competing at once.

Josie considered fleeing. Whatever business they had with Danny surely wasn't her concern. But before she could decide one way or another, all the men came tumbling out—seemingly at the same time, though the door couldn't accommodate their combined breadth.

"I can pay!" Danny keened. His face had been bloodied and his shirt was torn. "I can pay!"

"If you could pay," Nantz reprimanded him, "we wouldn't have to be here, now would we?"

"My things—"

"Trash," Carmichael sneered, stepping on a glass ampoule to illustrate his point.

With his hair falling over his eyes, and his waxed moustache flecked with spit, Danny chanced to look upon her.

"The girl!" he said, pointing an accusatory finger at Josie.

"What about her?"

"She owes me! *She* can pay!"

The triumvirate now faced Josie—Danny from his hands and knees, while his assailants loomed over him. The reek of desperation made her head swim.

"I fixed her boot," Danny appealed to Carmichael. "She gave me her I.O.U. Take that as payment!"

"Did you? Give him an I.O.U.?"

When Josie failed to respond, Carmichael rolled his eyes. "Did you spit in your hand or not?"

Unable to form a sentence, let alone give voice to it, Josie emphatically shook her head.

"Oh, Danny," Carmichael said. "Danny, Danny, Danny. You ain't an Irishman, are you? No honor, those lousy Irish." Then, wielding his cudgel, he brought it down on Danny's ankle, producing a terrible crunching noise and causing him to scream.

"She's my wife!" Danny shrieked. When this educed a momentary reprieve, he started to babble—rolling onto his back and clutching at his injury. "She's my wife—I've got the license to prove it! Just go inside and check—it's in my caravan."

Carmichael glanced at Nantz. "Say—how many's he made for you, Nantz?"

"Licenses? Three, at least."

"I've got one that says I married my dog." Resting his cudgel against his shoulder, Carmichael paused to reflect. "Not that I'd mind. She was a good dog."

"Belle?" Nantz asked.

"No, Lulu—the one before. Belle couldn't be bothered to lick her own a—."

Danny was still muttering to himself when the next blow caught him in the ribs. Josie felt weightless, her arms and legs buoyed by the air, as she watched the two men beat him to death. When he protected his face, they swung at his arms and legs. With every wound, Josie felt herself to be less corporeal, until finally she'd become a ghost, a silent, bloodless spectator. She never uttered a word; certainly, she never spoke in Danny's defense. Floating away, she felt herself rising up, up, up, past the branches and the laundry lines, up until she got snagged in the highest limb.

CHAPTER 15

The Sergeant Major had always favored his right hand. Since losing it, he'd favored his left hand or nothing at all.

Penmanship could be frustrating, if not messy (he frequently smeared the ink), but he managed—drafting endless inventories of Fort Brogue's supplies and writing letters to his younger sister, Clara, in Cincinnati, in which he joked about the awful weather. He parted his hair on the left, like the portraits of his late mother's father. He cinched his belt backward and trimmed his nails with his teeth. Most time-consuming of all were the tasks that required two hands, like lacing his shoes. More often than not, he was reduced to tears of frustration. But if one devoted sufficient thought to it, one could forecast an entire day. By doing so, the Sergeant Major hoped to identify any pitfalls and to plan around them.

If the evening meal were to be soup or stew (easily gleaned from the kitchen staff), he'd dine with his men; but if dinner would require the use of a knife and fork, he would dine alone. There wasn't any shame in having his food cut for him, but the association was that of a helpless child or a doddering old man. It was poor for morale, as well as for his self-esteem. Happily, soups and stews were a mainstay of the military. If it could be served in a cup, it could be served on the battlefield.

Another potential embarrassment was the necessity of saluting. In the U.S. Army, a soldier always saluted with his right hand, and a salute was always returned in kind. In order to avoid these situations, the Sergeant Major had refused every promotion put to him since the Battle of Vicksburg. For as long as he remained a non-commissioned officer, no enlisted man would be required to salute him; so long as nobody was saluting him, he didn't have to salute back.

Everything happened in sequence, each event the product of its circumstances. To wit, the day of Miss Josephine's disappearance had been ordinary from the start: breakfast alone, with his copy of the family Bible. Bound in white leather and embroidered with gold thread, the book was ostentatious but remained open of its weight, which the Sergeant Major found to be useful.

He was drinking coffee when he received the news: Miss Josephine was absent from her room, and no one knew where to find her. (Of the other turrets, not counting the Sergeant Major's and Miss Josephine's, a third housed Myers, and the fourth was reserved for guests, should a person be so misguided as to spend the night at Fort Brogue.) Absorbing this information, the Sergeant Major had thanked the dispatcher. And then, rather than hurrying, he'd calmly finished his cup—continuing to read until the Israelites had fled from Egypt.

Making his way across the parade ground, he encountered a half-dozen soldiers, running drills. The men's jovial encouragement was suspended while he passed them, everyone standing at rigid attention, so he performed his best Myers Walk—stiff-kneed, and leading with his chin. This was greeted by much hooting and derision, though he managed to maintain a dispassionate expression. Only after he'd passed did he allow himself a smile.

When the Sergeant Major arrived at Miss Josephine's turret, Harrison, the lieutenant who'd been assigned guard duty, was looking especially forlorn, his eyes fixed on the ground and his shoulders slumped to diminish his outsize height.

"Hello, Lieutenant," the Sergeant Major said, attempting to make eye contact. "I gather we've had an eventful morning?"

"Yes, sir. No, sir—I don't think. But that's why, sir—so this morning—"

"Why not take a deep breath and tell me what's happened?"

Stealing a glance at his superior, Harrison sighed. "Yes, sir—all right. So, last night was usual—Miss Josephine turned in before dark, and no one's come or gone since."

"And you were standing sentry this whole time? You're absolutely certain she didn't leave?"

"*Certain,*" Harrison replied, a little too emphatically. "All night long."

"And this morning?"

"This morning, when she didn't come down for breakfast, I went up to check her room. I didn't want to barge in, so I knocked and knocked, but there was no answer. Finally, I called to say I was coming in. And the room was empty!"

The Sergeant Major gave a curt nod. He'd seen enough in the past year to gauge the Lieutenant's aptitude, which he'd rate on the low end of the scale. However, it wasn't a lack of caring that made Harrison inept. He truly desired to be a soldier, even if he possessed none of the necessary attributes.

"Isn't it possible," the Sergeant Major now proposed, "that you fell asleep at your post?"

"No, sir, I never—"

"And isn't it also possible," he continued, "that Miss Josephine decided to go for a walk? Or, what does she call it—a lunt? Lunting?"

Harrison shook his head, as if to prevent the word from gaining purchase. "I don't know anything about that. Like I said, I knocked on her door and she was gone."

"Perhaps you're concerned about getting in trouble. I think it's time we had a talk, Harrison, about the importance of telling the truth—"

Upon hearing a bump, they both reacted

simultaneously, the Sergeant Major arresting his thought and Harrison glancing up the stairs. Typically, Miss Josephine had a light footfall—heavier if she were wearing riding boots. This sound had been ponderous, like the canter of a horse. It was followed by another, and then another, the sound echoing from the turret above.

"Harrison," said the Sergeant Major, his eyes never leaving the stairwell. "You're quite certain the room was empty?"

Opening and closing his mouth, the lieutenant stammered, "I—I—"

"Get men. Be quick."

"How many?"

"Three. Do it now."

He was gone and back in a matter of seconds, with three amiable recruits at his heels. They were unarmed, pulled from their training exercise, and for that the Sergeant Major was grateful; in such a confined space, a bayonet could be lethal; never mind the damage that a bullet could inflict.

Leaving the forlorn lieutenant at his post, they bounded up the stairs. The young soldiers stalled when they reached the door—kicking and slapping with their palms, until the Sergeant Major was able to force his way through. He hadn't visited Miss Josephine's quarters since she'd moved in. Initially, she and Myers had shared accommodations, an arrangement that no sensible person would've brokered. Once provided her own space, she'd seemed to be more contented. Doubtless, she'd found the turret room cozy enough, what with her mementos and collection of books. The Sergeant Major had meant to ask her for a recommendation, in fact—something that Clara might've favored, not knowing for himself what a girl might enjoy.

"Miss Josephine?" he now called through the door. "Can you hear me, Miss Josephine? Are you there?"

When there was no reply, he tried peering through the keyhole. The Sergeant Major could see the window frame, opposite the door, its view obscured by clouds. The room was rounded, with no feasible place to hide. Still, he could hear a vague scuffling noise, as if someone were moving just beyond sight.

Then he saw a figure that approximated a man, with deranged eyes and a hideously long beard. The fiend was nude, with skin the color of chaw spit, sunken cheeks, and a hairless crown. His shoulders and back were spattered with bird droppings. And though he was hardly more than skin and bones, his limbs were grotesquely long.

Horrified, the Sergeant Major fell back on his haunches. If Miss Josephine was inside, then her life was in peril. Possibly she was already injured, having been silent for so long.

"No one goes in there," he rasped, as the three other soldiers helped him up. He saw panic in their eyes, a desperate longing for his trademark assurance. Instead he ordered them, "No more pounding on the door. You do nothing—just make sure that nobody leaves. Do you hear me?"

Rushing down the stairs, he passed the lieutenant

on his way to the postern gate. The young man started, lost in thought. It made the Sergeant Major wonder: if someone had been fleet of foot, how likely was it that Harrison would've heard him?

"What? Where—"

"You stay there!" the Sergeant Major barked at him. "Just you wait!"

As always, the view beyond the postern gate threatened to leave him breathless—the vast and untamed continent coming to an abrupt end, with only a fingernail of sand to distinguish its shore. While the wind tousled his hair and blew up his trouser legs, the Sergeant Major followed the fort at right angles until he reached Miss Josephine's turret—little more than a ledge for him to stand upon, before the land dropped steeply toward the ocean. If the intruder hadn't climbed up the stairs, as Harrison claimed, he would've had to come from this direction. Clearly, the Sergeant Major wasn't expecting to find anything so obvious as a ladder, but it was necessary for him to check.

Looking up, he spied Miss Josephine's window, partially concealed by a bank of clouds. The perspective threatened to give him vertigo. From this angle, he could see where the weather had impacted the wood—the saltwater mist that drifted up from below, and the storms that arrived almost daily. What good was a fort, he thought to himself, no matter how steadfast, if it couldn't resist one man?

Retreating behind the fortifications, to where the wind was less pervasive, he sought out Harrison again.

Grabbing the lieutenant's shirt with his one good hand, the Sergeant Major hissed, "Don't you dare lie to me—you fell asleep on watch, didn't you?"

With a look of horror on his face, Harrison gushed, "No, sir, I swear! I didn't!"

"Did you even check upstairs? Because someone—*something*—is in that room with Miss Josephine, and he bloody well didn't fly in. So if he didn't come up the stairs, you tell me—how'd he get in there? *How?*"

Harrison was close to tears. His only response was a feeble shrug—which, insufficient though it may have been, forced them both to acknowledge the odd choreography: a one-handed man accosting a significantly taller youth. Thus anchored to the present, the Sergeant Major released his grip, absently patting Harrison on the chest. The lieutenant wasn't lying; at least, he didn't *think* he was. And despite how the turret had actually been breached, the fact remained: Miss Josephine had become someone's hostage. Nothing else mattered.

"What're we going to do, sir?" Harrison whimpered.

"Tell Myers," the Sergeant Major replied. "Call him back from town. And, by God, you're coming with me!"

"*Me?*"

"Yes, you," he snapped. "If the tempest rages, you're going to get wet."

From above, there came the sound of a minor disturbance, followed by a soldier tromping downstairs. It was one of the three eager recruits; the Sergeant Major couldn't tell them apart, for all their cockeyed enthusiasm.

"Sir!" the soldier reported. "The person's talking!"

"Talking?" the Sergeant Major echoed. "Talking, how? What did he say?"

The young soldier looked perplexed, not an uncommon state for the men. "I don't think it's English," he frowned. "I'm not sure if—"

At sufficient volume to penetrate the wood, and to rise above the howling wind, they could all hear the guttural reply, *"Leck mich am Arsch!"*

CHAPTER 16

When Frank Myers was still a young man, new to Manhattan and new to himself, he'd made a habit of buying the *Times*, the *Herald*, and the *New York Tribune*. How could he court opportunity if he failed to appreciate the world at large? God knows he hadn't slogged over from Scotland to lie in a pauper's grave. Every morning, he'd pay his two cents to the Greek at the intersection of Fulton and Pearl—a negotiated fee, the first of many.

"Today's news?" the Greek would ask in vowels that lilted and swooned.

"Have you tomorrow's? It's worth more to me."

"Today is tomorrow, yesterday. For half, you can have it."

Always, the same: *for half, you can have it*. Frank hadn't known the Greek's name, nor what sunny isle he'd hailed from, but in a city fast approaching a million he alone had recognized Frank by sight. Were Frank to have decamped for Boston, or to have enlisted in the Army, no one but the Greek would've noticed his absence.

But all this had changed when the Greek had been replaced. It had been a summer day, steam already rising from the pavement.

"Where's the other fellow?" Frank had asked the new vendor, palming his two bits. "The Greek—is he sick today or what?"

"Dead," the man replied. In his face, Frank could see the ruddy-cheeked youth he'd once been, now yellow-toothed and jowly. The man had done a poor job of shaving that morning, the whiskers still visible on his pale neck. "Hit by a brick, coming back from lunch. What d'you want, chum—the funny pages?"

"A brick from a building?" Frank winked, even as his pulse had quickened. "Or struck from behind, d'you mean?"

While he waited for the man to elaborate, two more customers purchased the news, reaching over and around him.

"How about his boy, then?" Frank persisted, when the vendor remained mute. "I'd see him sweeping up, now and again."

"What about him?"

"Shouldn't he be working this corner? By rights it's his."

"Oh, is it?" the man said, taking a step closer. "You

ever hear that possession's nine-tenths of the law? Well, this is the other tenth. Now either buy something or get moving."

Another customer jostled Frank from behind. He could feel his bile rising, but had somehow managed to tamp it down. "I won't be giving you my business," he seethed, "so I'll get moving, instead. But before I do, let me speak the plain truth. If this is the other tenth, then you're one-tenth the man."

"You get out of here," the man had snarled, planting a hand in Frank's chest and giving him a shove.

It was shortly thereafter that he'd decided to move west, maybe someplace with less ornate architecture, less prone to falling rubble. Looking back on it nearly two decades later, he could see what he'd most cherished about the Greek: the sense of continuity that the man had provided. It was why, when he'd opened his second Myers & Co. Store, Frank had copied the layout of the first down to the very last detail. Apples by the entrance, pickles by the register. Cigar cases opposite the counterman, behind glass, so that he could observe the customers' reflections.

It was also why, before decamping from the isle of Manhattan, Frank had paid a second visit to the ruddy-faced vendor, dragging a blade across his neck and leaving him to die in the street. Another summer day, steam rising from the pavement.

Were Frank to die today, he'd certainly do better than a pauper's grave—but what of his livelihood, for which he's sacrificed these many years? It would be sold off, part and parcel, with all the proceeds going to the state. If possession truly was nine-tenths of the law (as he'd seen proved out, time and time again), he obsessed over the one-tenth men and their base behavior. Deception could wear a friend's mask, or even a business partner's. Who would protect Myers & Co. after Frank had gone to meet his Maker?

His niece Josie was the obvious answer, an heir to all he'd accomplished. In the absence of a son, there was no better candidate to take the reins. Josie was fair, smart, and fearless—easily superior to any boy her age. Who else would've come to America, sight unseen, to be received by an uncle she only knew from his portrait? No doubt she could direct his business to places Frank even hadn't conceived of—not just the retail stores, but the lumber industry, too. What's more, it would provide her with financial security long after he was gone. The only obstacle was a matter of identity, his and her own. The one-tenth men would surely plunder her inheritance if Frank didn't safeguard it.

Thus, it was with thoughts of posterity that Frank exited the bowling alley and walked toward the congregation. More than a dozen parishioners were loitering outside the Methodist church, all of them dressed in their Sunday finery—and in their midst, Judge Harper, his bald head turning a shade of salmon. Frank waved and smiled as he passed familiar faces, even receiving the occasional handshake. But he didn't stop moving until he'd reached the circuit judge.

"Your Honor!" he said, intruding upon some

meaningless banter and causing the judge to confront him.

"Myers," he grunted.

"Enriching service, I hope?"

"Hard to hear," the judge remarked pointedly. "The reverend had to contend with a near-constant banging."

"Did he?" Frank grinned. "How lucky the Lord has fine hearing! I was wondering if we could speak about the Naturalization Act."

"Not now."

"When, then? Would next Sunday be convenient? Any excuse to practice my bowling."

As Frank patiently awaited his reply (trying his best to appear guileless), he took note of the crowd's homogeneity. Not a red, yellow, or brown face among them. No doubt a flock for whom citizenship had been all but assured.

"Five minutes," Judge Harper said, the collar of his shirt going limp from perspiration. "Next week, you practice on Saturday."

Satisfied, Frank nodded. "Agreed. Now, I haven't reviewed the document myself, but I've spoken with a lawyer who has. He informs me—"

"By law, a fourteen-year residency is required," the judge interrupted him, while investigating an itch in the depth of his armpit. "Not including the five-year notice period. I don't know when you immigrated, Myers, but—"

"The Act doesn't concern me. I'm curious about its provisions for children."

Frowning, the judge stated, "There aren't any provisions regarding children—not that I'm aware of."

"Not so. The lawyer I spoke to was very clear—"

"Foreign-born children of a United States citizen may also be considered citizens. The Fourteenth Amendment extends those privileges to anyone born inside the United States, regardless of their parents' place of origin. The Naturalization Act details penalties in the event of fraud. That's it—that's all."

It wasn't often that Frank found himself tongue-tied, or ill-prepared for an eventuality. As he attempted to process this new information, he was faintly aware of a commotion coming behind him, provoking the other congregants to turn and stare.

"Children adopted by a United States citizen," Frank recited from memory, "or children with a legal guardian—"

"Let me ask you something, Myers." A cruel smile spanned the judge's face. "This lawyer you spoke to . . . is he formally educated?"

"Of course."

"And where did he receive his schooling?"

"I'm sure I don't know."

"But you—you're not a lawyer, are you?"

Judge Harper delivered this inquiry while looking over Frank's shoulder, as did many of his coterie. Feeling compelled to turn around, Frank spotted Gordy and Gak moving toward him. The latter, in particular, looked incensed—her mouth screwed up tight, and her tiny hands balled into fists. Though Frank made obvious shooing gestures, Gak cleaved a path through the crowd, paying as much heed to the congregants as she would a herd of sheep.

With an exasperated sigh, Frank answered the judge, "No, I'm not a lawyer."

"Then perhaps you'll heed my advice. Your niece—I assume it's Miss Josephine we're talking about? Like you, her path to citizenship is abundantly clear. Fourteen-year residency. Five-year notice. Ensure that her paperwork is in proper order and she might be an American citizen by 1890. Who knows—maybe you'll even live to see the day."

"You welched, Myers!" Gak shouted, jabbing a finger at Frank and thrusting out her chin.

"Your Honor—" he petitioned, attempting to speak over her head. But there was no denying the obnoxious child, her fingers sticky with taffy and dangerously close to his face.

"You'd all but lost. You know it, I know it, even the Chinamen knew!"

Looking away from the judge, Frank registered the crowd's titillation. It was evident in their smiles, and how they craned their necks to see. After church services, these God-fearing men and women had only their Sunday dinners to captivate them; Gak was more entertaining by far. Consequently, she was pandering to her audience. While ostensibly talking to Frank, she also took a step back and projected her voice, so as to be overheard by the remotest pair of Christian ears.

"Now, I won't call you a liar and a cheat . . . only, you

walked away from a fair contest, and that's the opposite of fair dealing. You ducked what you had coming!"

"What I had coming?" Frank scoffed. "There was no wager, no stakes!"

"I may not know about running a successful business," Gak replied, with galling humility, "or mitigating expectations, but I'm no dummy, either. When a person wins, he gets something. And when a person loses, he loses something. Also, anyone who welches is nothing more than a cheat and liar."

With these words of opprobrium, she reached out to brush some lint from his shirt, a gesture that received raucous applause. Aware that a response would be required, Frank quickly considered his options. Gak had insulted his station; he could, in good conscience, strike her down. From the obvious efforts she'd made to conceal her gender, the majority of the crowd wouldn't recognize her as female—and even if they did, they'd be too cowed by Frank to voice their dissent. But what purpose would it serve, other than the satisfaction he would receive? Better to confound expectations, and be the bigger man.

Marshaling his ire, Frank affected a grin. "I've been called many things in my time," he laughed, also projecting his voice to be heard above the crowd. "Sometimes a cheat and a liar. But never a Welshman before!"

It was funny—not remarkably so, but funny. People chortled. However, they'd been more pleased to see this young upstart deriding a successful businessman; Frank's good humor only hampered their fun. And so, with their

Sunday dinners growing cold, the assembled congregants began to disperse—and with them, Judge Harper.

"I'll see you next week," Frank hollered after him, earning himself a look of reproach. "By which I mean Saturday, of course."

"She didn't mean what she said," Gordy apologized, when it was finally just the three of them. There was an edge to his voice, which Frank initially mistook for embarrassment. "She was only joking. Tell him you were joking."

For emphasis, Gordy shoved Gak—and for the first time Frank could see the fissure between them. It was evident in the downward cast of her eyes, and Gordy's tensed shoulders.

"No bother," Frank said. "I don't mind being the source of fun. But look here—it's the Sergeant Major. Let's see what he has to say about winners and losers."

Their circle opened to include two riders approaching on horseback, both similarly attired: formal blue tunics and leather riding boots. The younger of the two was Harrison, a lieutenant much taken with Josie, for whom Frank entertained a mild enmity. The Sergeant Major could be distinguished by his impairment. A Union veteran, he lightly grasped the reins in his left hand. His right sleeve, resting on the saddlehorn, had been neatly folded and tailored to a seam.

"Mr. Myers," the Sergeant Major said, not bothering to dismount. "I'm glad I found you."

"And I, you! Did you know, Sergeant Major, how Judge Harper would define an honest citizen?"

Almost imperceptibly, the soldier sagged. "I'm sure I don't care."

"Oh, but you should! After fighting so valiantly, and giving so freely of yourself! An honest citizen, according to His Honor, is a sheep. Not a wolf, mind you—not one who can hunt and fend for himself—but docile, with fleece as white as snow. Waiting without want or complaint, until he's led away to the slaughter."

"Mr. Myers—"

"Doesn't that vex you, Sergeant Major? Knowing that your nation was founded on laggards? That is, if Judge Harper's to be believed. If you ask me, I'd say his opinion is worth one-tenth your own."

"Be that as it may, Mr. Myers, I'd appreciate a word in private."

"Yes, yes," Frank conceded with a sigh. "State your business."

Glancing at Gordy and Gak, the soldier hedged, "It would only take a moment, if you'd like to—"

"Don't mind the rabble, Sergeant Major—spit it out!"

"All right. Like I've been trying to say—" Lashing the reins about his wrist, the soldier soothed his mare, kneading her flank with his one good hand. "Miss Josephine has been taken hostage."

With a bark of laughter, Frank rolled his eyes. "What do you mean, *hostage*?" he said. "Hostage to one of her moods? You know teenage girls, Sergeant Major."

"I'm sure I don't," the soldier replied. "And I mean exactly as I say. Confined to quarters with a hostile interloper. A Deutschman, I think—we can't see through the door, and he refuses to speak English. Now, would you care to accompany me back to Fort Brogue?"

"You're serious?" Frank could feel his stomach lurch—like that long-ago morning on Fulton and Pearl, the newsprint still tacky on his palms. The instinct to do harm was so pronounced he had to fold his arms to stay his hands. "She's really in trouble—my Josie?"

"Can I say it any more plainly?"

"I know some German," Gordy blurted out. Everyone turned to look at him. "You say he's a Deutschman? Well, I know a little."

"Then come with us," Frank declared. "You can ride with me."

"Me, too?" Gak asked.

Surprisingly, it was Gordy who answered her. "No," he snapped. "Not you."

There it was again, the fissure. Whatever tension existed between them, it wasn't far below the surface. Too fraught to be a lovers' quarrel, it had the feeling of something more intimate, something intractable. Though the greater portion of Frank's mind was now occupied by his niece (how best to subdue Josie's captor, and what manner of torture would be most appropriate), he was happy to facilitate Gak's comeuppance.

"What?" she protested. "No, I—"

"Your friend has spoken," Frank interrupted. "I have a need for him—but if he doesn't want you, then you're dead weight. For all I care, you can sod off."

"She's going to the Logging Camp," Gordy volunteered. "To find her daddy."

"Sergeant Major," Frank said. "Can your man escort her there?"

"Lieutenant, do you know the way?"

"Yes, sir," the young soldier confirmed. "Down the coast, sir."

"Good—commandeer another horse and take her there."

Suddenly, everyone was in motion.

"Now wait just a minute," Gak insisted, but no one appeared to be listening to her. Frank and Gordy had started walking toward the stable, and the Sergeant Major had steered his mare around. When the lieutenant dismounted from his horse to offer her a boost, Gak batted him away.

"Gordy!" she said. "I'm talkin' to you! Let's all of us go together, so we can find your uncle. Then maybe afterward, we can—"

"*My* uncle," Gordy cut her off. "Not yours—*mine*. I don't need your help—I've had enough of that already. Go and help yourself for a change." With that, he continued toward the stable.

Before Gak could respond, Frank brought his face close to hers—so close that her eyes went crossed. "What's done is done," he said—able, at this proximity, to smell taffy on her breath. "Now run along by your lonesome self. And the next time you accuse me of welshing, just remember I pay my debts." Withdrawing a step, he added, "Good luck finding your daddy."

CHAPTER 17

Through the aperture of the keyhole, Froelich eyed his captors. He was mindful not to stand too close, lest they be tempted to jab something at him, but he could see them even from a distance—their cheeks shaved, like a grotesque mob of babies. They spoke English in a variety of accents, too fast for him to comprehend, and banged on the door with the flats of their hands. Yet another reason to stand back, lest they take the thing off its hinges.

Ever since he'd woken to find them, these man-babies had remained a constant bother. It seemed they were trying to communicate with him; moreover, Froelich got the impression they wanted him to leave. Not one to suffer the yoke of authority, he was inclined to ignore them, but for the fact that he was otherwise trapped. So the man-babies continued to stare at him, while he continued to stare back, and little was done to resolve the situation.

When he wasn't engaging in mutual surveillance, there were other pursuits to occupy his time. He'd already experimented with lying down: the bed, perhaps a little short for his legs, had been as soft as a mother's embrace. Now that he was fully rested, he'd also experimented with sitting on the mattress. The position required nothing of his arms and shoulders, and very little of his legs, besides. Occasionally, one or the other of his buttocks would go numb and he'd have to massage it to regain sensation, but otherwise Froelich enjoyed the decadence—a state of leisure he'd rarely been afforded while supporting himself on the rungs. But always the man-babies would bang on the door again, disturbing his tranquility and making him feel harried.

"What is it?" he yelled, keeping his back turned to the keyhole. "What do you want? I've got no candies for you!"

They wouldn't be satisfied until he'd left, and if he were going to leave it would have to be out the window. Thus, raising himself up from his seated position, Froelich limped across the room to look outside. The herd of clouds continued to graze on the turret, happily producing their bleating noises. If he were going to escape, he could ride one of them to freedom. Only, this time, he might pick an older steed—not a baby, like before, but one of substance and heft. No more fear of the bottom collapsing, or of being digested over time.

Truth be told, the idea of piloting a cloud didn't

appeal to him. Froelich wasn't confident he'd be able to steer it, which begged the question: where would his new cloud take him? Out to sea, obviously, but what coast beyond the distant horizon? Not the Deutschland of his youth, he hoped; that sad and desolate place held no more appeal to him now than it had upon his departure. Less so, without Harald by his side! How pitiful everything would seem, minus the company of his brother. Who would deride the pig farm, if not the two of them together?

"Not today," Froelich said, reaching out the window to pet a downy flank. "Maybe some other time I'll ride you. For now, my two feet are comfortable on the ground."

The window still offered a means of egress, cloud or no. To the untrained eye, the turret may have appeared smooth—slick, even, as a result of the ocean spray. But Froelich could distinguish seams in the wood, and depressions where the moss was masking irregularities. Testing his grip against the window pane, he knew he'd be able to climb down, his fingers made vise-like from years on the rungs. But even if he managed his descent without injury, where would he go when he reached the bottom?

Peering down from this vantage point, Froelich was reminded of Sir Knost's ladder, the third tallest in recorded history. As boys, he and Harald had traded tales about knights of the Teutonic Order, playacting their exploits. Sir Knost had been a favorite of Froelich's, a minor knight known for his vanity. When a lord of the

Lithuanian highlands had declared his daughter to be off-limits, even going so far as to have her sequestered, Sir Knost had conspired to woo her.

After arriving in the highlands, Sir Knost and his squire had visited a nearby grove, wherein they'd discovered a remarkably tall tree. In medieval times, knights had used escalades to scale castle walls. More often than not, these escalades had been constructed from whatever materials were available on hand. But before Sir Knost was able to chop down the tree, a wood sprite had emerged.

The timber belonged to him, the wood sprite explained, but he'd exchange it for a lock of Sir Knost's hair. The knight agreed to these terms and set to work. The tree was exceptionally tall, as was the resulting escalade—so tall, in fact, that twice Sir Knost compared it to his storied manhood. (His squire, a pimply boy of twelve, suffered these jests in silence.) Finally, when their labors had been completed, the wood sprite returned to receive his payment, but Sir Knost reneged on his debt, threatening the creature at swordpoint.

Fleeing, the wood sprite cursed the escalade and anyone who would scale it. But Sir Knost would not be deterred. Up he climbed, until he felt he should've reached his good lady's window—and still he'd climbed. Up and up, until it seemed like he'd been climbing for hours. Up and up, until afternoon became night, and he was forced to sleep on the rungs. Only when a new day had dawned did it occur to him that enchantment was afoot.

Henceforth, it hadn't mattered if Sir Knost climbed up or down: the rungs had extended endlessly in either direction and no breach in the wall would ever appear. The days had grown shorter and the seasons had changed. Sir Knost had aged, and his gorgeous hair had fallen out. Worst of all, he'd become lonely. When more time had passed than he cared to recall, he let go, plummeting to his death. His companion, who'd witnessed the whole affair, would later swear that he'd never climbed higher than the twentieth rung, nor had an hour elapsed. Sir Knost had lost his wits, and nobody mourned his passing, least of all his pimply-faced squire.

But now the man-babies were hammering on the door again, causing Froelich to start. With a rueful laugh, he stepped back from the window.

"It's unwise to yell at someone so close to the edge," he barked. "Such a person might be tempted to jump!"

Outside, his captors continued their protests, honking and bleating. The sounds they made were frightening, Froelich would admit to himself, as was their hideousness—but were they even real? Or were they the product of another fever?

Keeping his back turned, he elected to sit at the writing desk. It had been years since he'd last occupied a chair, and he spent a few minutes admiring its construction: like a miniature ladder, only with the rungs and stiles arranged differently. Though his left buttock went numb almost immediately, he found that he enjoyed the respite—leaning back, and taking the full weight off his feet. Idly, he scanned the surface of the desk: some mementos, paper and an inkwell, and a fresh quill.

In that moment Froelich decided: he would not leave this place. Maybe it was real, maybe not. Maybe, climbing out the window, he would fall to his death like poor Sir Knost, or find that he'd fallen off the ladder some time ago, and only now lay sensate at his brother's feet. But for as long as this delusion persisted, with the squalling man-babies outside his door, he'd appreciate the perks it had to offer, be they lying down or sitting up. He only had to explain his absence to the one person who might notice. Thus, choosing a piece of paper from the top of the pile and inking his nib, Froelich thought for a moment before composing his first sentence to Harald.

CHAPTER 18

The Logging Camp had grown since Gak last saw it, this being her third visit in four years. Venues like the Chinese laundry and the smokehouse had erected plywood walls, steam issuing from tin chimneys like pale vines. It was hard to say how large the camp had become, since its borders remained undefined and were veiled in a constant fog—certainly big enough to warrant a charter. But who among these lost souls would petition for such a thing? If any of them desired a social contract, they were welcome to find it elsewhere.

As Gak traversed a familiar network of footpaths, she reflected on the previous day's events: Carmichael and Nantz, the jitney driver, and finally Francis Myers. The one constant had been Gordy, and now he'd forsaken her. Kicking a toadstool, she tried to summon indignation, in the hopes that it might enliven her, but all she could feel was a deep and abiding shame. Gak had been no safer as a boy than as a girl—in fact, she'd been a danger to others! If not for Gordy, she'd be dead twice over; as a result of having saved her, he wanted her gone. It was impossible to reconcile. As it was, she had too much ground to cover and too few resources at her disposal.

Cresting a low hill, to where a brook ran shallow beside a half-dozen campsites, she recognized a face. Zyke's Menagerie had been given a wide berth by its neighbors, most of them sleeping under tents, with a few covered wagons parked alongside. Approaching the lonely caravan (its gilding leached of vibrancy), Gak could see why.

"Hey, Owen," she called out. "Nice bear."

The rotund man looked up from his breakfast and blinked at her. Whatever fate had befallen the original Zyke, he'd borne no relation to Owen—nor, Gak imagined, had he shared the same rheumy eyes. When he chewed, Owen betrayed an allowance of rotten teeth. The menagerie, won in a poker game, boasted no more than five or six animals at a time, whatever he could trap himself.

One time, Gak had helped him catch a feral pig, but even that was relatively tame compared to a bear cub. The bear in question was small, but still larger than Owen. She wore a conical cap, affixed by a chinstrap, and bangles that chimed when she moved her paws. Otherwise, she was unbound, no more a captive than anyone else. Sitting on the opposite side of the campfire, her damp fur stinking something awful, the bear exhibited all the signs of human despondency.

"Is that you, Gak?" Owen said. "I almost didn't recognize you. Yeah, thanks—she's all right."

"Is she? Because she looks kinda sad."

"She's had a rough go of it, lately."

"Where's the monkey?" Gak asked, looking around.

Gesturing at his companion, Owen replied, "She ate him." Immediately, the bear emitted a piteous groan.

"Not the monkey!" Gak said. "I liked him!"

"So did she. You might even say they were the best of friends. But these things happen."

"I suppose so," Gak agreed, surreptitiously eying the bear. "Say, Owen, have you seen Gaylord?"

"Can't say that I have. You asked Harmony?"

Gak scowled. "I was hoping not to."

"If you're looking for Gaylord, that's where I'd start. But now that I got you, Gak, can you spare some money?"

"I'm afraid not."

"Oh—okay. Spare a cigarette, then?"

Reaching into her pouch to oblige him, Gak tried to muster a sympathetic farewell. In her experience, Zyke's Menagerie had always prospered. A bear was no small attraction, literally or figuratively. And if Owen needed something more exotic, he was sure to find it. But none of this was easy to convey, in the all-too-obvious absence of the murdered monkey.

"Feel better," was all that Gak could manage, with an apologetic wave of the hand. In response, Owen nodded his head. The bear just moaned.

Gak proceeded through the camp at a deliberate pace. It had been half a day since she'd arrived. Her escort, the prodigal lieutenant, had seemed distraught when they'd parted ways, not wanting to abandon her in such company, but he'd been gone by morning. Hopefully, he'd returned to Fort Brogue, though Gak might stumble upon him here—uniform bartered, mares too, making strange new acquaintances out in the woods. The Logging Camp could suck a man in and swallow him whole. But if that had indeed been the lieutenant's fate, it was none of her business. Someone else could intervene, or neglect to intervene—whichever.

She would've liked to have found her daddy first thing, but it had rained overnight. The storm had turned everyone inward, faces cowled and camaraderie shunned. Passing the night in her preferred hollow tree, Gak had found the candle she'd secreted the year before, but rodents had filched her boiled pine. It had been more than a day since she'd eaten—which was good, she thought. It made her ornery, a deterrent to the lecherous type. Despite her treatment at the hands of the jitney driver, Gak had been protecting herself for years. When she'd first come to the Logging Camp three summers ago, she'd spent half her time warding off solicitations. It helped that she'd changed her appearance since then. At eleven she'd still been wearing bloomers, with hair that she'd groomed like an exotic pet.

Now, coming upon Harmony, Gak was hardly surprised that she'd acquired a roof. Given her profession, it was best not to expose herself to the elements, or poor business sense at the very least. Harmony was standing outside her shanty, leaning against the door and sipping a cup of coffee. There was a heavy wool blanket wrapped around her shoulders, to stave off the chill. Underneath it her ankles were bare. Gak had no choice but to approach her directly, subject to the madam's scrutiny for the last twenty paces.

"Well, look at you. Last time you was here, you was just a girl."

"Last time I was here, you was under a john."

Narrowing her eyes, Harmony said, "Makes no difference—standing up or lying down. Either you see things plainly or you don't."

Before Gak could answer her, a man pushed past—flashing his purse in Harmony's face before disappearing through the door. The madam didn't acknowledge him. Instead, she took another sip from her mug, her painted lips leaving a mark.

"I guess you'd know," Gak said. "Spending so much time on your back."

"If that's what you're after, I can help you next."

Feeling an irrational flush of shame, Gak attempted to change the subject. "I'm here for my daddy. Have you seen him?"

"Harmony!" the man shouted. "I'm ready!"

"I doubt it," she muttered. Turning to peek inside, she instructed the customer, "Take off your shoes and socks."

As the man cursed and grumbled, Gak repeated the

question: "Have you seen him or not?"

"Gaylord? Maybe. Why should I say?"

"Because I'm asking."

But it wasn't good enough; the look on Harmony's face was the opposite of cowed. Fighting back the urge to scream, Gak took a deep breath.

"Because if he was your kin, you'd be looking for him, too."

Initially, the madam's expression revealed nothing, and Gak despaired of a better option. But then she chortled. "You think? I wouldn't be so sure."

"D—n it, woman!" her customer harangued her. "I'm about as ready as I'm gonna get!"

"Honest," Harmony continued, "I haven't seen him in weeks. You know where the Chinamen pour their lye? If he's here, that's where you'll find him."

Gak left before the customer could be serviced. She trusted that Harmony was telling the truth: the smell of lye could be unbearable, but not to one who'd abused his senses. Plus, it would drive regular folk away. What better guarantee of one's desired privacy?

When she got to the prescribed place (as was made clear by the smell), she found precisely what she'd been looking for. Entering the radius of a dying campfire, the sound of a dinner bell caught her ear. The proprietor of the smokehouse would sound the chime whenever business was slow that he might whet the camp's appetite. But the tenants of this particular campsite, represented by two bundles of burlap, didn't seem to have noticed.

"Hey, mister," Gak said, prodding the one on the

right by kicking his feet.

Hawking a glob of phlegm, the man rolled over, only to burrow more deeply into himself.

"Hey, mister—your missus is here."

The words had the effect of a splash of cold water: sitting bolt upright, he let loose an empty clay jug. From his person wafted the scent of urine.

"She went that way," Gak gestured with her thumb.

Sure enough, the fellow loped off in the opposite direction. The ploy was so predictable, and so perfunctory, that just once Gak wished to see it fail. Sniffing the air to ensure he'd mostly peed himself and not his environs, she settled into the cavity he'd left behind, the ground here a bit more cozy and less damp than its surroundings. Reaching for her tobacco pouch, she hailed the other sleeping form.

"Mind if I borrow a spark?"

When he didn't answer her, she inserted a wick of rolling paper into the embers. It was prudent of Gak to save matches—plus, the smoldering paper served a dual purpose. Lifting it to her cigarette, she took a deep breath and exhaled with relish.

"Much obliged."

Then she flicked the wick, such that it landed between his chin and shoulder—muttering to herself, "Oops."

At first, he swiped at his neck, like he was trying to stave off a mosquito. When that failed, he tugged at his collar, as the wick wheedled its way past layers of clothing. Finally, it settled on a dry patch, and Gak's daddy came to life, hissing and paddling his chest like he was trying to revive his heart. This performance lasted a matter of seconds, after which time he became aware of her presence—still seated across from him, earnestly puffing on her cigarette.

"Hi there, Gaylord."

She gave him time to reorient himself. Reaching for the clay jug, so recently abandoned, she braved a sniff. Whatever they'd been drinking, it was enough to make her eyes water.

"You feelin' okay?" she said. "Like you're gonna be sick? When's the last time you ate something?"

Slowly batting his eyelids, he stared at her with middling comprehension, or so Gak assumed. Even bundled in rags, it was apparent that he'd lost weight. The last time she'd corralled him, after she'd lifted him to his feet, he'd been sick down the front of her shirt— nothing but sticky, green bile. Now he looked too wrung out to spit. For all his squalor, though, his fingernails were remarkably clean—gleaming in the half light like pearls in the dirt.

"I know you?" he croaked.

Despite his febrile state, he was staring straight at her. For a moment, Gak wondered if he was joking, or else foisting a lie. But there was nothing in his eyes to suggest humor, nor did he seem capable of guile.

"You don't recognize me?" she said, a sickening feeling taking hold.

Leaning forward, her daddy sneezed. "I'll share a smoke, if you got one."

With trembling hands, she dug into her tobacco pouch for a piece of rolling paper. What did it matter, she asked herself, if he couldn't see past her clothes and bruises? So what if he thought she was a boy—all it required was a few curt words and he'd know her true self. At the same time, was that what she wanted? Or who she wanted to be? When she couldn't hold the pouch steady, she gave up, dusting stray flakes from her fingertips.

"I'm nearly out," she faithfully reported, but Gaylord just continued to stare. "See for yourself," she said, tossing the pouch in his direction. "Ain't nothing but dust."

Wetting his lips, he asked, "What about—?" Making a tippling gesture, and pointing at the jug.

"Empty. You got your friend to thank for that."

There was a speech she'd been practicing since springtime. In it, she'd cite Dolly, Hollis, and Ma—how they were all waiting for him, at their genuine peril. She was going to remind him of his responsibilities, both as a husband and a father. But now she found herself drafting a new speech, which she could deliver upon her return home. She'd describe the bowling alley, the hollow tree she'd slept in, and maybe even Owen's bear, for Hollis's sake. Of this person before her, she'd make no mention.

But before she could excuse herself, and much to her surprise, her daddy flashed a grin. "Ah, heck," he grunted. "Nothing to smoke and nothing to drink—you'd think we was in church!" Despite all else, his smile still evinced a handsome face. When he clapped his hands together, Gak inadvertently flinched. "I'll tell you what," he said. "*Good*. Good, I say! There comes a dawn you wake to a fresh start, and I'm glad it's here. You say I don't know you? Then you don't know me. But loan me a dollar, friend, and I promise you this—come back tomorrow and you'll find me good as new. New prospects, new clothes, just a whole new man. What d'you say? Help me back to where I belong?"

Was there a flicker of recognition in his eyes? Or perhaps a tremor of contempt? Gak was equally content not to know. Rising to her feet (with a tingling sensation in her extremities, like she'd been held too long underwater), she peered down at him.

"Here's where you belong," she said. "You don't need any help for that. Who's got a dollar, anyway?"

Turning, she took the first of many steps away from him. But she'd only made it a few strides, her pins-and-needles feeling greatly improved, when Gaylord threw himself at her feet. He couldn't have weighed more than a hundred pounds; the impact hardly caused her to lose her balance. Still, Gak jumped as if bit.

Without stopping or bothering to look back, she ran until her lungs burned. A glance in the opposite direction confirmed that she wasn't being pursued, Gaylord being too weak to give chase. Panting, she came to a stop. It was time for her to depart this place, Gak decided, hopefully never to return. Presumably, Gordy was still looking for his uncle. It was obvious that their relations were strained—you couldn't be a party to murder and still remain collegial. But Gak owed him her life. Though he'd denied her help, her debt to Gordy remained unpaid, and she'd been raised to pay her debts. Ironically, it was Gaylord who'd taught the lesson.

And so she resolved herself to go to Fort Brogue. If Gordy wasn't there, at least they'd know where to find him. Just now, as the proprietor of the smokehouse rang the bell again (having failed to entice a crowd the first time), Gak's stomach rumbled in kind. Maybe she'd stop for a bite to eat, to gird herself for the journey. But then, as she was coming around the corner, she heard one Confederate voice say—

"I swear, I can eat so much bacon, my belly'd come out to here!"

—and halted in mid-stride. Furthermore, upon hearing the rejoinder—

"If your belly was any bigger, Carmichael, I'd mistake you for the pig hisself!"

—all her intentions were swept away, like so much scum on a moonlit river.

CHAPTER 19

Once the cookfire had burned down, and the silence between them had assumed a timeless quality, Miss Sarah became visibly restless. Having already cleaned the area around the base of the ladder, she now gathered the breakfast dishes and stuffed all her wares into her wicker basket. Watching her, Binx was moved by the desire to say something—to thank her for her charity, at the very least. But the import of Froelich's philandering, as well as the Rübezahl's departure, had left him feeling despondent.

"I've been meaning to ask," Miss Sarah finally said while chastely folding her napkins. "What's that?"

"What's what?"

"That," she clarified, pointing at the fulcrum. The large and ungainly piece of furniture was resting on the far side of the meadow, draped in the shadows of the dogwood trees.

"It's a fulcrum," Binx explained, rubbing a muscle in his thigh. "Harald carved it, for balancing the ladder."

"How *old* is it?"

"As old as the ladder. They've both held up pretty good, don't you think?"

Laughing, Miss Sarah admitted, "I thought it was a wheelbarrow without any wheels." But then, as she parsed his words, her expression changed. "Wait—what do you mean, for *balancing the ladder*?"

The weight of the stiles made it all but impossible to shrug, but Binx managed a rough approximation, raising his eyebrows and turning out his palms. "Just as I say."

"You mean you don't have to stand here?"

Dropping her basket, Miss Sarah stalked off to the far side of the meadow, bunching her apron in both hands. Binx was surprised by her sudden urgency, and more than a little confused, but he contented himself to watch her in silence. Running her hands over the soft wood, she thoroughly examined the fulcrum's surface. No matter the distance between them, Binx could've described every inch of it—every nick and detail. He and Gordy had spent countless hours on its steep planes, scampering up one side and sliding down the other.

"Do the wheels work?" Miss Sarah called, raising her voice above the birdsong.

"They should. But it's heavy," Binx added. "I doubt you can move it."

Putting her shoulder to the fulcrum, she immediately proved him wrong. Though Miss Sarah was able to persuade it a couple of feet, she would've had an easier time lifting one end and taking full advantage of the wheels—advice that Binx was reluctant to dispense.

"I can't believe it!" she exclaimed, standing and wiping her sleeve against her forehead. "This whole time, it's been here?"

"I don't see the big deal," Binx huffed. "Just because you never noticed it—"

"Don't see the big deal? Binxy—*you can leave*! You don't have to stand here! Why haven't you ever walked down to the river, or gone into town, or even decided to take a little nap?"

The impertinence of these questions made his cheeks feel hot. As if he'd never considered the possibilities. Why did everyone think he or she knew better than Binx—that somehow he had trouble making decisions for himself?

"It's a poor substitute," he informed her, though he found it difficult to meet her gaze. "For a person, I mean—the wood doesn't yield if it gets windy, or if the ground's hard with frost. And what if Froelich needs something? What if he sends a message down the rungs and I'm not here to listen?"

But even as he said this, he realized his mistake: Froelich *wasn't* up the ladder. His uncle's absence struck him anew, causing his jaw to clench. Binx *could* leave the ladder unattended without there being any consequences—except, of course, he couldn't. His responsibility went beyond Froelich's safety; there was a principle at stake.

Walking back toward him, Miss Sarah smiled in infuriating fashion. "I'm not saying you should leave it forever—perish the thought! Only, can't you take a short break? Is that really such a bad idea?"

In addition to being unable to shrug, the stiles made it impossible to turn away. He could only cross his arms and stare into the distance, trusting his reticence to speak louder than words. What he wouldn't give for Lord John, Binx thought, to come clambering down the rungs and question Binx's priorities. Hadn't the Rübezahl claimed to be listening? Would there be a more appropriate time to make himself known?

"Fine," Miss Sarah said, collecting her bonnet from the ground. "I'm sure you're right."

"Of course I am," Binx insisted. "Don't you think I've given it some thought?"

"Obviously you have."

"I'm responsible for the ladder," he continued. "I can't just walk away because I feel like it. This is a serious responsibility! Harald built the fulcrum, but even he hardly ever used it. If he'd wanted the ladder to lean against it, he would've asked for the fulcrum when he died, instead of telling me—"

Seeing the look on Miss Sarah's face, Binx arrested himself in mid-sentence.

"Binxy," she said. "I'm sure if Harald were here, he'd say it's okay for you to take a break. He built the—the fulcrum, you said? Then I'm sure he wasn't opposed to using it. That's like building a door, and telling everyone to stay inside! If you've been standing here this whole time, for however many years, because you think you might disappoint him—"

"Harald's dead," Binx interrupted her. "You can't disappoint someone who's already dead."

"You can't impress him, either."

The truth landed with the weight of Froelich's chisel. Even the breeze faltered, abandoning the leaves with a tremendous sigh. Binx stared at the bonnet in Miss Sarah's hands. How long would he continue to support the ladder, in the hopes of securing his father's praise? Ten years? The rest of his life? While he pondered this thought, his body, always so insistent for his attention, continued to itch and to ache. Stonily, he tried to focus on the stiles, whose faint tremors reached him from even the highest rungs, where they warped and swayed in empty space.

"You couldn't move it the rest of the way by yourself," he finally rasped, attempting a dry swallow. "The fulcrum's too heavy. You'd have to wait for Gordy."

"Yes, Gordy," Miss Sarah replied, sounding chastened. "Anyway, he's the reason I came. When will he be back?"

Binx snorted. All these years he'd sacrificed to the ladder, and his brother was free to come and go. In that respect, he was no better than Froelich!

"Who knows?" he spat. "Probably never. He could be dead, for all I know! More likely, he's off having himself a ball while I'm stuck here. I wouldn't depend on

Gordy, if I were you."

Stuffing her bonnet into her apron pocket, Miss Sarah nodded. "No—I won't. Too bad," she added. "I could've used his help."

"What for, did you say?"

"To slaughter a pig. Hiram's no use."

"What makes you think Gordy is any better?"

The idea seemed to catch her off-guard. Miss Sarah paused for a moment, then gave a slight shrug of her shoulders.

"There's other stuff he can do, besides. Feeding the animals, rebuilding the wall—like I said, Hiram is useless. To be fair, his talents lie elsewhere, but it's hard work running a farm."

Picking up her basket, Miss Sarah prepared to leave, even arranging her bonnet back atop her head. In that instant, Binx decided not to worry about Gordy, nor would he trouble himself with Froelich. Apart from balancing the ladder, Harald had taught him one other thing: how to butcher a hog. After all, he'd been heir to the family farm before departing for America.

"You think you can move the fulcrum?" Binx asked.

Miss Sarah blinked at him, her basket dangling from her elbow. "That's what the wheels are for, right?"

"I can help on the farm," he said. "Just promise that Hiram will leave me alone. No more questions about the ladder. At least, not right away."

"I can't speak for anyone else," Miss Sarah said, crossing the meadow and applying her shoulder. "But I'll ask him."

The fulcrum proved surprisingly easy to move, once it had gained a little momentum. They had some difficulty maneuvering it into place, making sure the rungs were properly aligned; but after it had been positioned opposite Binx, he could nudge the ladder against its steep plane. The stiles made a trough in the dirt as they rotated over the axis. There wasn't any need to worry about Froelich, or how he'd handle the transfer; the Rübezahl, if he even existed, could fend for himself.

Standing upright and taking a wobbly step forward, Binx expected to feel a soreness in his legs; after all, two years had passed since he'd straightened his knees. There was a profound dread associated with this moment, and the memory of seeing Harald collapse to the ground. Paradoxically, then, Binx experienced a lightness in his joints, minus the weight of the ladder, as if he might somehow float away. It was a ludicrous prospect, one that made him giggle nervously.

"Are you all right?" Miss Sarah asked, sounding concerned. Extending her arm to him, she proposed, "Do you need something to lean against?"

"No, actually, if you could just—"

Knowing she couldn't reach as high as his shoulder, Binx placed her hand on his forearm. Miss Sarah frowned, but left it there regardless. The pressure of her palm, no bigger than a maple leaf, allowed him to feel grounded.

"Like that?"

"Yes," he said, with a shaky sigh. "Like that. For now."

He didn't glance up at the ladder, or look behind

him. For a short while, they made no effort to move. They just stood there, feeling the sun on their backs, as the smile on Binx's face grew wider and wider.

CHAPTER 20

A tumultuous night had passed since Miss Josephine's abduction. During that time, Gordy had stuck to the periphery of things, learning what he could from stray bits of conversation. No one had seen or heard from Miss Josephine since the Sergeant Major's discovery, nor had the Deutschman made any demands. To a man, the soldiers were baffled as to how he'd managed to enter Fort Brogue. Meanwhile, Myers was calling for a military tribunal—for the Deutschman, the sentry, and anyone else who might've been remotely culpable. Despite all the calls to action, the state of affairs was largely unchanged.

Though he'd kept his own counsel, Gordy had suspected Froelich's involvement from the start. First, there was the matter of the Deutschman's nationality. Second, upon their arrival, he'd noticed the soggy wad of clouds clinging to Miss Josephine's turret. If indeed his uncle had been poached by one, the wind would've blown it in this direction.

"I know a way to get him down," Gordy helpfully suggested. He and the Sergeant Major were standing outside the fort, peering up at the turret through an overcast morning. When not barking orders at his men or consulting with Myers, the Sergeant Major could be found here, staring at the window and fingering his Remington. The pistol had been a constant accessory since the day before, always holstered at his hip.

"He can flap his wings, for all I care," the Sergeant Major muttered, turning up his collar against the sea breeze.

"I mean safely."

"No one wants him down safely. If the Deutschman can be apprehended without any harm to Miss Josephine, it's not so he can live out his days."

Though Gordy had suspected as much, it was another thing to hear it confirmed. Froelich (presuming it *was* Froelich up there) had little chance of surviving, should Fort Brogue's mood remained the same. He had no means of escape, and no food to sustain him. Unless Gordy could effect a change on the ground, there was only one way for the situation to end.

"Why is Myers so hell-bent?" he asked. "He says we should have a trial. He said, show a man a noose and he'll find it hard to breathe."

"A trial? There won't be any trial."

"Why not?"

"Because you can't have a military tribunal for a private civilian," the Sergeant Major tut-tutted, his eyebrows raised. "If it's justice Myers seeks, I can summon Judge Harper—not that Myers would suffer the insult. Still, unless he can find a suitable replacement, all of this"—here, he waved his good hand at the turret—"is mere pageantry."

It wasn't the answer he was looking for, but Gordy decided to drop the subject. There was another question he'd been harboring: why was Myers so distraught about his niece? You'd think she was his daughter, from how he carried on.

"Can I trouble you one last time?"

"You want to know about my hand?" Grunting, the Sergeant Major said, "It's not like you think."

"I don't think anything," Gordy promised.

"Of course you do—everyone does. It was the last night of the Vicksburg siege. Do you know where that is? We knew that Pemberton was going to surrender— he'd already written to General Grant, stating his terms. Between that and the next day being the Fourth of July, we were all giddy with anticipation." Suddenly, the Sergeant Major glared at Gordy. "This ladder of yours— it's not here, is it? He couldn't have used it to climb up there?"

"Where do you think I'd hide it," Gordy scoffed, "in my pants? Anyway, your hand—did it get exploded or shot off?"

"All I ever wanted was a scar, something to show the pretty girls. If that sounds idiotic—well, I suppose it is.

Anyway, I got a good look right before she bit me. She fell right into my hand."

"She?"

"A fiddleback spider," the Sergeant Major said. "Not so nice to look at, but dainty. The color of an acorn, and not much bigger. She landed in my palm, and—oh, bloody hell!"

The wind had changed directions, delivering a minor squall to where they stood. As water blew at them sideways, like someone emptying a bucket, the two men found themselves drenched. Retreating back inside, they left the turret window to its lonely view. For his part, Gordy felt on the verge of articulating an idea—something about what the Sergeant Major was saying as it related to the current situation.

Eager that he not lose the thread, he implored, "So you lost your hand to a spider bite?"

"Fiddleback," the Sergeant Major repeated, as if the distinction were paramount. Standing just inside the postern gate, he borrowed from a pile of horse blankets to dry himself off. "If you don't believe me, go ask someone—they can kill a cow, and bigger things. When she bit me, it hurt worse than anything I'd ever experienced. Worse than getting burned, worse than being shot. The next morning, thirty thousand Rebels got paroled all at once, all of them hoofing it to Alabama. By the second day, I couldn't extend my fingers. By the third day, when I finally found myself a doctor, it had turned black. There wasn't any discussion—he just took it off. People tend not to ask how it happened, and I don't say."

"Isn't that the same as lying?"

"A lie of omission?" The soldier smiled. "How about I answer your question with a question? Which hand do you use to pick your nose?"

Gordy frowned. "Pick my nose? My right hand, I guess."

"But you had to think about it?"

He had, though it put him in a different mindset than the soldier had intended. Maybe Myers wasn't bereft over the loss of his niece, Gordy realized; maybe he was grieving for his own right hand! All at once, Gordy saw a way out—for himself, for Froelich, and even for Miss Josephine, should she so desire. Not bothering to dry himself off, he made a hasty apology:

"Sorry, Sergeant Major—I gotta find Frank!"

Not waiting for a reply, he ran across the open parade ground, crossed to the opposite turret, and bounded up the stairs. Gordy expected to find Myers at Miss Josephine's door, and so he did. The Scotsman made an indecorous sight, squatting and peeking through the keyhole. At the sound of Gordy's approach, he stood abruptly, smoothing his shirt with an air of embarrassment.

"Yes?" he demanded. "What is it?"

"Miss Josephine was going to be your right-hand man!"

"Not so loud," Myers hissed, casting an anxious glance at the door. "He may not know that."

"But she was, wasn't she? And now she can't? That's what the circuit judge was saying—she won't be a U.S.

citizen for another twenty years?"

"*Nineteen* years," Myers automatically corrected him. But this exchange had the effect of focusing him, such that he stood a little taller. "You overheard all that?"

"I did," Gordy nodded. "I'm always listening, hearing what other people have to say. And I'm creative, too— like at the bowling alley! You didn't think I could win, did you? But I did, and not by changing the rules, either. Like you said, I mitigated expectations. Am I right?"

"Not entirely," Myers frowned. "But you've got a keen ear, even if you failed to grasp my meaning. So what? What does any of this have to do with my Josie?"

"Me! Make *me* your right-hand man! I'm smart, I'm motivated—plus, I'm already an American citizen!"

The idea was still new to Gordy, but he was confident of its merit. For this reason, his was disheartened by Myers's response. In the confines of the narrow stairwell, the Scotsman's laughter bounced off the walls, almost like a trapped bird.

"Oh-ho, it's a job you're after? I should've guessed it, shouldn't I? Well, Mister Right-hand Man, maybe you can answer me this, since you're so motivated. If I were to employ you, how would you resolve the current situation? Surely you've got an answer, being as creative as you are."

"Easy," Gordy said. "Froelich's my uncle."

All the Scotsman's good humor, no matter how fatuitous, promptly vanished. "Your uncle?" he croaked.

"I'm pretty sure—mostly sure. Anyway, it's not like I lied." Borrowing from the Sergeant Major, Gordy qualified, "Or if I did, it was a lie of omission. I'll just knock on the door and tell him to let her go. That's what you want, isn't it?"

"No."

Frowning, Gordy peeled his shirt from his chest. It was becoming unpleasantly stuffy in the stairwell, and his clothes, still wet from the recent downpour, smelled altogether brackish.

"No? What do you mean, *no*?"

Shaking his head, Myers muttered, "The man's demented—he's naked and ranting, locked away in a tiny space. What if you knock on the door and he doesn't believe you? *I* can hardly believe you, and I've still got my wits about me. It's too easy."

Desperate to press his advantage, Gordy blurted out, "I have a ladder."

The idea was so tailor-made that it actually made him smile. Myers, however, seemed unconvinced.

"A ladder?" he echoed, cocking his head to one side. "You're saying you've got a ladder tall enough to reach that window?"

"The fourth tallest in history—seventy meters, at least. It'll reach Miss Josephine's window and keep on going. It's not here, obviously—I'll have to send word to my brother to bring it, and he'll need help, but we can have it here in a day or two. If Froelich won't walk through that door, you can go in the other way."

"A ladder," Myers said a second time, clearly at a loss for what to think. "And you'd be prepared to give it to me?"

"I'd sell it to you."

"*Sell* it?"

"Well, I don't work for you yet, now do I? You said if I had to choose between money and fame that I should always choose money. This ladder could make me famous. There's a reporter from Philadelphia who wants to write about it. But you," Gordy added, looking the Scotsman in the eye, "can do better than a newspaper story. You can make me your right-hand man. It's an easy decision."

A moment of silence passed between them. In the distance, the sound of the surf rose and fell, and beyond that came an ethereal disturbance, like the tinkle of wind chimes. While waiting for his answer, it suddenly occurred to Gordy that Myers would research his history—that he'd hire someone like cousin Hiram to investigate his past. Indeed, why would a magnate trust his affairs to a total stranger?

Finally, the Scotsman thrust out his hand. Staring at it, Gordy expected to feel elation. But instead of sealing the pact, he remained with his arms pressed against his sides. His mind had returned to that country lane, littered with mail, and the victim he'd left by the side of the road.

"Do you not see my hand?" Myers barked, seemingly oblivious to his duress. "Take it, man! Don't let an offer wither on the vine!"

Shaking his head, Gordy said, "Frank, there's something I have to tell you before I can shake. Something I've done."

In his mind, he was furiously unspooling the narrative, trying to find its natural starting point. Not riding on the mail jitney with Gak. Earlier, then—as far back as Carmichael and Nantz? Or further still, when he was falling through the trees? All his thoughts, Gordy discovered, terminated with the ladder.

Myers's outstretched hand had flagged a little, but he'd managed to keep it extended. Perhaps to ease the strain on his shoulder, he now took a step toward Gordy and reached out, seizing his palm in a firm grip.

"I can see it weighing on you," Myers said, holding Gordy's gaze. "This terrible thing that you've done? Take it from me, lad—we've all done terrible things. All of us, without exception. But the only alternative is *not* doing bad things when the moment requires it, and that has consequences too, does it not?"

Gordy was picturing the jitney driver, his pants pulled down around his ankles, sprawled over Gak. Up until this moment, he hadn't allowed himself to consider what might've happened next, had he failed to intervene. It might've been Gak lying dead in the road if Gordy hadn't swung his bludgeon.

"Let the one-tenth men debate the finer points," Myers continued, as if he were privy to Gordy's innermost thoughts. "In that way, they're trapped in the moment of indecision. We made our play, you and I—we did what needed to be done. So no more talk of deeds or misdeeds, yes? I won't hear another word. Now could you *please* rid my turret of your blasted uncle?"

Pumping Gordy's arm, Myers jarred him from his

revelry. Although he'd promised to deliver his uncle, Gordy wouldn't sacrifice Froelich's safety.

"Rid him, sure," he repeated. "But do you promise not to hurt him? No tribunal or firing squad—nothing like you said?"

Shrugging, Myers groused, "Of course—you have my word. So long as my Josie is returned safely."

Then, as if amused by a clever turn of phrase, a smile graced the Scotsman's face. "By golly," he said, tousling Gordy's hair. "I always imagined myself having a son!"

CHAPTER 21

After witnessing Danny's death, Josie spent hours wandering among the caravans. Carmichael and Nantz saw fit to let her go—or perhaps they made threats to ensure her silence; Josie was too distracted to notice, ever conscious of the hole in her boot. Whenever her thoughts drifted toward that awful memory, she stuck her toe in the breach, as if she were a dinghy taking on water. Finally, when the daylight failed her and it started to rain, she was forced to consider her sleeping accommodations.

Surely, she thought to herself, the Logging Camp must employ a prostitute, if not two or three. She didn't trust any man to offer her lodging without demanding something in return, not even one of the camp's missionaries. The brothel itself was easy to find. She spotted the hutch at the center of things, with Harmony loitering in front, even despite the presence of a steady downpour.

"You with squirrel?" she asked, before Josie could introduce herself. Up close, the madam's lips were painted the color of pomegranates.

"Am I what?"

"With squirrel. I can fix that." Her eyes drifted to Josie's midsection, giving meaning to the expression.

"Oh, no!" Josie exclaimed, horrified. "Not that! I just need a place to stay. I haven't got any money. I've made a terrible mistake, really, and I just—"

"Your shoes." Harmony's eyes flitted to Josie's feet.

"Pardon?"

"You can stay till morning, but only for your shoes."

"They've got a hole in them," Josie confessed. Inexplicably, tears filled her eyes and she suffered a bout of nausea.

The madam shrugged her shoulders. "There's worse things. If a caller comes during the night, you've got to wait outside. Understood? Unless you want to put some money in your pocket."

Rather than answer, Josie promptly removed her shoes—hoping the blush would quit her cheeks by the time she had them off.

Luckily, the eventuality of a customer never came to bear. Josie survived the night, albeit on little sleep, and in the morning the rain was slightly improved. She was eager to return to Fort Brogue; she only wanted to fill her stomach before quitting the camp. How hard could it be, she thought, to find a warm meal?

But now, guided by the clarion call of the dinner bell, she was all turned around. The last time she'd heard it, it had been at her back, meaning she'd either passed the smokehouse or her ears were playing tricks on her. Her eyes, too: in a place with more head lice than walls (not counting the tarpaulin), it was ridiculous she couldn't *see* the cookfire! She could've asked for directions, but even a whiff of helplessness might've been construed as something different. Frankly, she would've rather climbed a tall tree than submit herself to another wink, overture, or lewd grin.

Having lost all sense of direction, she decided to follow her nose, and finally she discovered what she'd been looking for. An uninspiring feat of carpentry, the smokehouse reminded her of a stable, save for the enticing aroma. Harmony had praised the brisket; and while Josie might've expressed misgivings, her way of thinking had changed.

"Hey!"

The voice came from behind her. Walk on, she thought to herself, determined to ignore it. It's just a vagabond, trying to provoke a response. Or another cobbler who's not a cobbler.

"Hey, red—over here!"

Spinning on her bare heel, she turned to face her aggressor—this vile little creature who would seek to rile and intimidate her. But when she looked, there was nobody there. Instead, she was presented with the broad side of the smokehouse, where the proprietor (busy at the moment, catering to a handful of diners) could enter and exit through a latched door. Frowning, Josie continued on her way. But almost immediately the voice sounded again.

"Here! Over here!"

From behind the door, a disembodied hand emerged, waved, and was swiftly withdrawn. That it appeared to be uncallused and possessing all of its digits confounded her expectations. With a sigh, Josie trudged over—peeking through the doorjamb, while being sure to keep her distance.

The air inside the smokehouse was kept artificially warm and poured out like something molten. Through the breach, Josie could see a boy approximately her own age, partially undressed and drenched in sweat. His face was the color of a turnip.

"What're you doing in here?" Josie asked, feeling her throat constrict.

"I'm roasting—what's it look like I'm doing?" When his sarcasm was greeted by silence, the boy moaned, "I'm *hiding*, you dummy."

"Hiding? Hiding from what?"

"From those two, over there." Pointing an index finger through the crack in the door, Josie observed a heat rash down the length of his arm. She did not, however, turn to see whom he'd indicted. "The fat one and the skinny one? If they see me in here, I'm as good as dead!"

Her first thought was that he was exaggerating; but then the image of Danny's face floated before her eyes, and she probed for the hole in her boot—realizing that she was now barefoot. As Josie herself began to sweat (the pores on her scalp opening up like tiny pinpricks), she thought to ask the obvious question:

"Why not run?"

"Because they'll see me!"

"Then why not stay here? Until they're gone, I mean."

"*You* get in here," the boy quipped. "See how you like it. If I hang around any longer, I'm gonna turn to jerky!"

Trying to keep her composure, Josie swiped at her brow. "Then what shall I do?"

"Cause a distraction! Go over there and get their attention. Then, while they're watching you, I'll sneak away!"

"Cause a distraction?" Josie echoed.

"Yes!"

"No."

The boy frowned at her. "Why not?"

Why not, Josie thought? Because she didn't enjoy being gawked at, which was precisely what the men would do—wasn't that reason enough? Or perhaps because this boy, whom she didn't remotely know, would presume to give her orders? Or maybe because these hypothetical fellows, who would so readily cause another person harm, might not lose interest when she was done *distracting* them. Any one of those reasons might've sufficed; but instead of choosing, she asked, "What's your name?"

"My name?" he scowled. "Why?"

"Because I'd like to know. My name's Josie."

As the rash advanced even farther up his neck, the boy made a vile noise.

"*Gak?*" Josie repeated.

"You heard me. So?"

"So?" she huffed. "Obviously it's not your real name, *so*. It's a common courtesy to introduce oneself—especially when asking another person for help. And why should I help you, when all you've done is be rude to me? Why not leave you here, to melt in a puddle?"

It could've been a result of his prolonged exposure, but the boy (Gak?) had turned an even deeper shade of red. While waiting for his apology, Josie nakedly appraised him. Unwilling to remove all his clothes, he'd rolled up his sleeves and pants legs to reveal long, sinewy muscles. The bruise around his eye made him look like a bandit.

"Gabrielle," he muttered.

"I'm sorry? I didn't catch that."

"My name's Gabrielle. My brother, Hollis, he likes to call me Gak."

"Gabrielle." With a sharp nod of her head, Josie said, "All right—good-bye."

"Wait!" he shouted after her. "What d'you mean, *good-bye*? You're not going to help me?"

"No, I'm not," Josie hissed, whipping around and finally venting her frustration. "Why should I, when you've made a mockery of me. *Gabrielle?* What do you think I am, some kind of idiot? I swear, if I didn't think they'd hurt you—"

"Good grief," Gak sputtered. "It's my name, okay? I'm a *girl*."

For a moment, Josie was at a loss. "A girl?" she said— though, once clued to the fact, it was possible to see.

"They'll kill me, all right? I'll *die*. If you don't do this, then I don't know what else."

Whatever misdemeanor Gak might be accused of, Josie had seen how justice was meted out. She couldn't feign obliviousness.

"Do they know you're a girl?" she asked.

"No," Gak said, vigorously shaking her head.

"All right then . . . wait here."

Before Gak could protest, Josie had already turned and left, in possession of an idea.

She found Harmony outside her hutch, in the same pose as before—a disheveled sentry manning her post. Befitting the early hour, she held a steaming cup of coffee.

"You decide to earn some money after all?"

Josie scowled at the suggestion, determined not to be intimidated. "I need some clothes."

The madam shrugged, absent any judgment. "What kind of clothes? I ain't giving back your boots."

"Girl clothes."

"For you?"

"For my friend."

"This friend," Harmony said, lighting a cigarette. "Is she your body type?"

"I don't see how it matters."

Exhaling, she shook out her match. "Different clothes fit different people, differently. You want your friend to look nice? Else we can stick her in a poncho, for all it'll keep her dry."

She was right, of course. Josie's ruse would rely on

Gak being disguised; to dress her in ill-fitting clothes would defeat the purpose.

"She's—" Thinking back to the smokehouse and Gak's state of undress (largely concealed from sight, but not to Josie's imagination), she attempted to do her justice. "Shorter than me, but with longer legs. Narrow hips. Not buxom, but pert—good posture, my mum would've said."

"Sounds ravishing," Harmony smirked, picking a coffee ground from between her teeth. "This friend of yours."

Josie understood that she was being teased. "Spare me your humor," she snapped. "I don't have any money, but my I.O.U. must be worth something. Otherwise, I can buy my poncho elsewhere."

"No one's taking your I.O.U., not when it's plain to see you ain't staying. Don't pretend elsewise." Giving Josie a once-over, she added, "I do fancy your dress, though."

Not two minutes later, Josie was back where she'd started—differently attired, and bearing a partial wardrobe in her arms. Her tastes had run more conservative than the madam's, but together they'd been able to reach a compromise.

"I'm not wearing that!" Gak insisted, as soon as she saw Josie's wares.

"Oh, yes, you are. They think you're a boy? Then we'll dress you like a girl. Now take off those rags—your trousers smell like meat."

"Is that a bonnet? I'd rather be caught dead!"

"Isn't that the idea?" Josie thrust Harmony's laundry

through the crack in the door. "Look, if you want my help, here it is. But don't think I'll spend another minute arguing."

Just then, the dinner bell rang. Gak stripped off her remaining clothes without another word and stepped into the dress. In the dim confines of the smokehouse, she looked like a trussed bird: naked, pink, and hopping on one foot.

"What'd you trade it for, anyway?" she said.

Averting her eyes, Josie stammered, "Clothes—my clothes."

"You traded clothes for clothes? Why not gimme yours instead?"

"Because yours smell like bacon. Hurry up!"

But Gak was having some difficulty with the buttons, unaccustomed to this type of garment. "Who'd you get it from?"

"Does it matter? The camp's madam."

"Harmony? You mean these clothes belong to a whore?"

"It's not the outfit that makes the woman," Josie sniffed, opening the door and tugging on her wrist. "Or haven't you heard?"

Together, they broke into a trot. The uneven ground pummeled Josie's naked feet, making it difficult to run—exposed roots assaulting her arches. For her part, Gak seemed too preoccupied to notice, running with a skirt bunched around her thighs.

The shouting began before they'd made it twenty paces:

"Hey, you!"

Immediately, she recognized the voice. It was Carmichael, who'd struck the initial blow to Danny's ankle, and Nantz couldn't be far behind. Without bothering to confer, the girls ran even faster.

"Slow down, you two! We jus' wanna talk!"

They could hear the sound of plates and utensils being dropped, followed by indiscriminate steps. It was like being stuck in a terrible dream, where Josie was running as fast as she could, knowing she was bound to be caught. They made it another twenty paces before a wheezing mass of gentility blocked their path.

"Couldn't you hear me? I said, slow down."

Like she'd thought (just like she'd *known*), it was Carmichael—grimacing and panting, his dinner napkin still tucked into his collar. Next to him, no worse for wear, was Nantz.

"Tell me, Nantz," Carmichael said. "Did I, or did I not, ask them nicely to wait?"

"You did, Carmichael," Nantz replied.

"Did you hear me say it? For them to wait?"

"I did. I could hear you plain as day."

Having established this fact, Carmichael peered into their faces—smiling, for all his benign toothiness, like a feral animal. Through her panic, Josie felt a small measure of relief that Gak had consented to wear a bonnet. With her short hair concealed, much of her would-be masculinity had been transformed. Even the bruise around her eye was hard to distinguish, given the unnatural flush of her skin. But the way that Carmichael

230

was staring at them, nothing could be certain.

"You," he said, rudely poking a finger in Josie's face. "Danny's missus. What's the matter with your friend? Why's she all red?"

"Leprosy," Josie answered, the lie taking flight so fast there was hardly time to think.

It was the first and only word she'd spoken to the Confederates, relying on nods and shrugs the last time they'd met. And what a word it was: Nantz leapt back, as if the syllables themselves might be infectious. But Carmichael only clucked his tongue.

"Nah," he murmured. "I've seen it before, at a colony outside Baton Rouge. It don't look nothing like this."

Josie was prepared to defend her falsehood when Nantz commanded in a hoarse voice, "You . . . say something different. Say something again."

"What—" she stammered.

"I knew it!" Snatching the dinner napkin from Carmichael's neck, Nantz yelled, "You're *Irish*, ain't you?"

"Actually," Josie frowned, "I'm not."

"Oh, yes, you are—don't be lying!" Dancing an agitated jig, he somehow seemed both delighted and distraught at the same time. "Where's the rest of you? Where there's a Irishman there's bound to be scores!"

Only here, in Oregon, would Josie have to differentiate between Ireland and Scotland. Despite everything else, she felt a desperate loathing for all things American—a loathing so urgent, in fact, that she was about to correct his mistake when Gak found her tongue:

"You said it!" she hollered. "Irishmen everywhere! In the bushes—in the trees! But mostly above you, in the trees!"

She was making an effort to disguise her voice, sounding high-pitched and squeaky. Not that it really mattered. The content of her message (if not the delivery) had been sufficient to spook the two men, such that they tripped over each other's heels, eyes wide and heads tilted back.

"Do you see 'em? I can't see 'em!"

"They're in the trees, Carmichael! Oh, it ain't right—I only just got dry!"

"And leprechauns, too!" Josie added. For this embellishment, she garnered a stern look from Gak—though why it should be any more or less preposterous, she couldn't guess.

"Leprechauns, Nantz! Protecting their gold!"

"I only just got dry!"

"There's one on your shoulder!"

When Gak failed to specify *whose* shoulder, each man assumed it to be his own. As they alternately slapped and pawed at each other, Josie and Gak slipped away, moving deliberately at first, until they felt confident enough to run. From the diminished quality of the furor behind them, they could tell they weren't being followed. And soon the ruckus had been lost to the trees.

"This way," Gak said, pulling Josie by the wrist. "Owen'll hide us. We can stay in his caravan till nightfall, and maybe get something to eat, besides. No one's gonna test that bear."

"What bear?"

They were still running, despite the fact that they weren't being chased. They were also holding hands—a boon to Josie, as she was stumbling in her bare feet. Gak's palm was warm against her own. Josie felt faint of breath, exhilarated.

"What?" Gak gasped.

Coming to an abrupt stop, they turned to face each other. "You said something about a bear," Josie insisted. "Don't tell me I'm going deaf!"

"Where're you headed?"

The suggestion caused her to flinch, as if this moment weren't a destination unto itself. She didn't want to go back to Fort Brogue, or to Uncle Francis. She only wanted to remain with Gak.

"I don't know," she said. "Nowhere."

"Me neither."

A pause elapsed between them. Then, as if the Confederates were still in pursuit, they started to run again.

"I can't believe we fooled those two," Josie laughed. "I can't believe it *worked*!"

"I know," Gak agreed, throwing off her bonnet. "Lucky for us you're Irish!"

CHAPTER 22

Froelich was stumped. A full day had passed since he'd started his letter, and still he didn't know what he wanted to say. Save for completing this chore, there'd been little else to occupy his time, confined as he was to his solitary cell. He'd slept, he'd read, and he'd sat with his legs crossed. But no matter how he'd distracted himself, the letter still needled him.

It seemed abrupt to open with his departure from the ladder, almost childlike in its bluntness, so he cast about for harmless platitudes. *How are you? How's the weather?* Somehow, questions such as these, asked for the sake of asking, seemed *more* offensive. Surely there was a happy medium to be reached, between bombast and bromides? Staring down at the mostly blank page, he hummed along to the sound of the clouds.

Dear Harald,

That was all he'd managed so far. He'd wavered on the "Dear" part; even now had misgivings. As inspiration, he tried to imagine his brother opening the letter, ripping the envelope with a look of stern concentration. How would he feel, when he first recognized Froelich's handwriting? How did Froelich *want* him to feel? It was as good a place as any to start: determine the emotion he meant to elicit, and work backward.

The truth was, it was impossible to imagine Harald opening the envelope when there were no envelopes to be found. Not on this end table that doubled as a writing desk, not under the mattress, or tucked among the bookshelves. Anyway, who would deliver it, provided that Froelich could locate an envelope? And how would he address it? *To the large man standing underneath the very tall ladder?*

Stabbing his quill in the inkwell, he rose from his chair. The turret room (which he'd come to think of as his own) wasn't ideally suited to pacing, given that it was small and circular, and yet he engaged in this futile exercise—crossing to the door, where he confirmed for the umpteenth time that nobody was peeking. Meals, Froelich had discovered, were delivered twice daily, once in the morning and once in the evening, discreetly left outside his door. He didn't question this arrangement any more than he'd questioned riding on a cloud; indeed, some things were best left unexamined. It was midday, hours yet until his dinner would arrive.

Thinking of eating, he was suddenly reminded of an incident from his youth—and, just like that, Froelich had found his platitude.

Stalking back to the writing desk, he took up his quill and added:

Do you remember Hermann the pig? I haven't thought of him in years—how he used to follow us around like a dog, and how we called him Hermann the pig-dog. Poor, old Hermann the pig-dog—I wonder what's become of him. (I don't know why I asked that; we both know what's become of him.) Do you think he pined for us when we left? Probably not. He probably spent his days contentedly, like the mindless creature he was.

I was specifically thinking of the time you fed him streusel kuchen, and the awful mess he made. Do you remember that, Harald? He was no fool, Hermann the pig-dog—he knew you'd share your dessert with him if he badgered you enough. We should've called him Hermann the pig-badger! I still recall the sounds that he made, following you all around the farm and even inside the house. And, oh, the mess—the mess that he made—when you finally gave him a bite. Do you think it was the cinnamon that roiled his stomach? Or the cloves? I'd never seen a pig with diarrhea before, and hope never to see one again. But the sight of you cleaning up all that mess, with a rag in one hand and your kuchen in the other—

Smiling, Froelich replaced his quill in the inkwell. He hardly expected streusel kuchen to be served with his evening meal, but the memory had caused him to salivate: the delicate balance between savory and sweet, especially when the recipe called for chopped walnuts. Wondering if Harald ever ate so well under-rung,

Froelich's thoughts turned to Lotsee, and immediately he felt a stab of resentment. In his mind he could picture her, as beautiful as when he'd first seen her. For too long, he'd fought the urge to say something—to utilize his TAP to its fullest extent. Instead, he'd patiently waited for Harald's apology. With that behind them, they could've traveled again! Or stayed in Oregon Country, where he could've been an uncle to Harald's boys. And so he'd waited too long, his stubbornness getting the better of him.

Froelich glared at the page. Here was something he could write: *Why did you choose her over me? Yes, she was bewitching, but was that worth your brother's love? Or did you think I sulked these many years because* she *chose you? Don't be ridiculous! To imagine I'd spend decades up a ladder because of that! I'd already forgotten her name by the time I'd reached the double-rungs. But you, Harald—your betrayal I have not forgiven.*

Outside, the clouds jostled against one another. A sea breeze blew through the window, shuffling the pages on his desk. When he felt in better command of his emotions, Froelich reached for the quill.

I am in a comfortable place now, Harald. I'd like to share it with you, but I doubt you'll ever come here. There's a bed, and ample books, many of the classics we enjoyed in our youth. I'm well fed, and there's a view of the Pacific, such that I might've seen from the ladder. It was never my intention to leave, you know—a hungry cloud made that decision for me. But now that I'm free, I can see I overstayed my welcome. If you're still there (and where else would you be?), I hope that you've noticed my absence, and that you'll lay the ladder down. It was the one thing between us—for better or worse—and it's not between us anymore. I would very much like to see you again, but I don't think that's possible. Instead, I will try to imagine you somewhere else, without that weight upon your back.

Do you remember Deutschland, Harald? I do. Not just the parts that made us leave, but the good parts, too—like Hermann the pig-dog, and streusel kuchen. Silly things. I remember being chased by bees, and how you'd sing The Song Without Words—the one you made up, which you'd hum to me when I got upset. Or waking in the middle of the night and not knowing what time it was, whether closer to midnight or closer the dawn. Hearing you breathe, Harald, and realizing you were awake, too. Wondering how much time we had like this. If I didn't squeeze your hand then, in the dark, imagine me doing so now. Imagine my voice, brother:

I am here with you, Harald. We are not alone.

EPILOGUE

From the highest rungs, the earth curved and the air moved like a body of water. Time passed in lazy increments: spiders spun elaborate webs, untroubled by the prospect of an errant foot, while birds nested under the clouds' reach. Froelich's seasonal garden turned wild, with the introduction of mint and lemon balm. In his absence, life between the stiles flourished.

Down below, Binx joined Miss Sarah on the farm—as part-time help, at first, and later as a permanent fixture. His knees had been damaged by years spent supporting the ladder, making certain chores impossible, but mostly he enjoyed the labor. He also made it into the newspaper, albeit for unexpected reasons. When his nine-pound onion won first prize in a local competition, Binx's name appeared in the *Oregon Spectator*, along with his likeness.

Gak left the Logging Camp and returned to her family's boarding house, accompanied by Josie. Nobody challenged the new arrival; on the contrary, Dolly wanted to know the latest styles in Europe, while Hollis mimicked her accent. As for Gak's ma, she remained circumspect—fixing a guest room when Josie arrived, which she restored to normal after the bed went unused. Gak only mentioned Gaylord once, to explain that she couldn't find him.

Gordy excelled as Frank's right-hand man, visiting Myers & Co. locations far and wide to inspect their inventory and layout. With all his traveling, he rarely returned to Fort Brogue, and gave little thought to his uncle. Gordy never provided Frank with the ladder; there hadn't been any need, once Josie wrote to reveal her whereabouts. Froelich stayed in his turret, Myers & Co. named a new successor, and the ladder was left undisturbed.

Until one day, a new tenant arrived: a lad from Boxboro, sent by his mother to collect chanterelles. He chanced upon the meadow with his eyes trained down. Lotsee's cottage had long since collapsed, so any sign of human habitation was missing—save for the immense, free-standing ladder, which he only noticed when he passed beneath its shadow.

Looking up, the boy's eyes grew wide. He circled the ladder three times, paying special attention to the fulcrum—how it supported the stiles, and how its wheels might be employed; moreover, how it resembled a massive wedge of cheese. Once he was confident that the arrangement was stable, he stepped closer. His mother had always accused him of being cautious, but now the boy was overcome by curiosity. Reaching out, he gripped the ladder with one hand: immediately, a vibration trilled down his shoulder, as if he were touching a living thing. The boy tilted his head back, but couldn't see an end to the winnowing stiles. Chanterelles forgotten, he kicked off his shoes and started to climb.

About the Author

Jamie Duclos-Yourdon, a freelance editor and technical expert, received his MFA in Creative Writing from the University of Arizona. His short fiction has appeared in the *Alaska Quarterly Review, Underneath the Juniper Tree,* and *Chicago Literati,* and he has contributed essays and interviews to *Booktrib.* He lives in Portland, Oregon.

Acknowledgments

I owe my gratitude to the following people:

My mom and dad, who encouraged me from the start. Without them, nothing would've reached the page.

Jennifer Finney Boylan and Aurelie Sheehan represent a legion of patient teachers. Julie Barer, Sarah Branham, Jenni Ferrari-Adler, Jud Laghi, and Vera Wildauer all contributed their time and professionalism.

The members of the Guttery, my immediate literary community—specifically, David Cooke, Mo Daviau, Susan DeFreitas, Tracy Manaster, Beth Marshea, Lara Messersmith-Glavin, A. Molotkov, Brian Reeves, Kip Silverman, and Tammy Lynne Stoner. Unaffiliated but no less appreciated are Ramon Isao and Tye Pemberton.

Yelena M. Dasher, Alex Minkow, and Jon Wasserman are my first readers and (by now) hoarse cheerleaders.

Laura Stanfill for her vision and enthusiasm. Gigi Little for her transcendent cover art.

And, finally, Melissa Duclos, without whom I wouldn't have tried.

FROELICH'S

LADDER

A

READERS'

GUIDE

1. Josie's tower is reminiscent of the story of Rapunzel. What other myths or cultural references did you spot within the pages of *Froelich's Ladder*?

2. Author Jamie Duclos-Yourdon said the following about his impetus to write *Froelich's Ladder*: "The characters compelled me to write this book—I couldn't shake their sense of alienation. Much has been written about the isolation fostered by or exacerbated by the rise of the Internet, but people have always suffered from loneliness. Moreover, people have always reached out to one another. Froelich's ladder is the central metaphor in the novel, but each character ultimately finds him- or herself alone, up the proverbial rungs, waiting to feel the slightest vibration." How does the theme of alienation play out in the novel?

3. Has Gordy helped or harmed Binx by enabling him to stay under-rung for so long? How about Miss Sarah?

5. Is Froelich a godlike character? Why or why not? Does your answer change once the author allows us into the character's head?

6. There are three murders in *Froelich's Ladder*. What does each incident tell you about the characters who did the killing? Are any of the murders justifiable?

7. What do you make of the Rübezahl's presence on the page?

8. *Froelich's Ladder* is hard to classify. It's a literary novel with fabulist elements. It's also historical, a traditional comedy, and could be considered neo-Victorian (contemporary fiction that evokes nineteenth century styles while retaining a modern approach to issues). Are there any books that remind you of this novel? What are some of the similarities or differences between those books and *Froelich's Ladder*?

9. How does the theme of gender play out in *Froelich's Ladder*?

10. Compare and contrast the two sets of brothers in regard to each one's sense of loyalty. Do you blame Harald for ruining Froelich's chance at happiness—or was Lotsee, for Froelich, another dream that was bound to have flaws, just like his impulse to move to America? Why doesn't Binx set down the ladder instead of taking his father's place? Does the loyalty Gordy and Binx have to each other and to their uncle stem from their father's sense of obligation to his brother? What about Gak's loyalty to her family?

11. By the end of the novel, each of the characters has paired off with another character. Name the pairs. Who remains alone, and why?

12. How does Francis Myers's approach to business relate to the American Dream and wanting to get ahead? Do you like Uncle Frank? Why or why not?

FOREST
AVENUE
PRESS

To invite author Jamie Duclos-Yourdon to your book club, by phone or in person, contact him through his website, jamieduclosyourdon.com.

Forest Avenue Press titles are distributed to the trade by Legato Publishers Group. Linda Kaplan of Kaplan DeFiore Rights represents foreign rights. For more information, see forestavenuepress.com.